THE WIZARD OF WARSAW

Note for libraries: A catalogue record for this book is available from Library and Archives Canada at https://collectionscanada.gc.ca

ISBN: 978-0-9952778-9-2

MW Books
Garden Bay, BC
Canada
http://mwbooks.ca

Katarzyna Wasylak

THE WIZARD OF WARSAW

In collaboration with

THE JANUSZ KORCZAK
ASSOCIATION OF CANADA

chapter
I

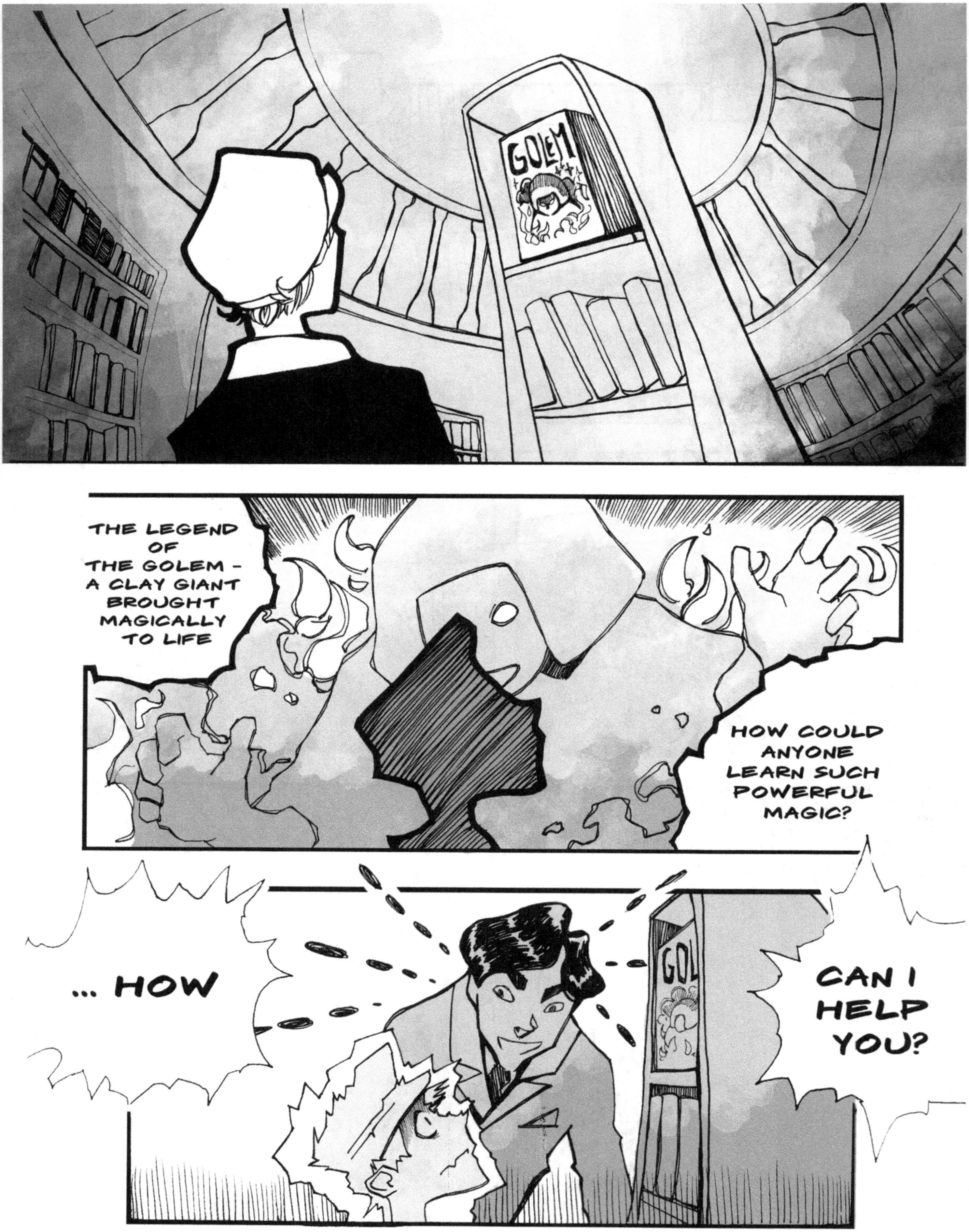

THE LEGEND OF THE GOLEM — A CLAY GIANT BROUGHT MAGICALLY TO LIFE

HOW COULD ANYONE LEARN SUCH POWERFUL MAGIC?

... HOW

CAN I HELP YOU?

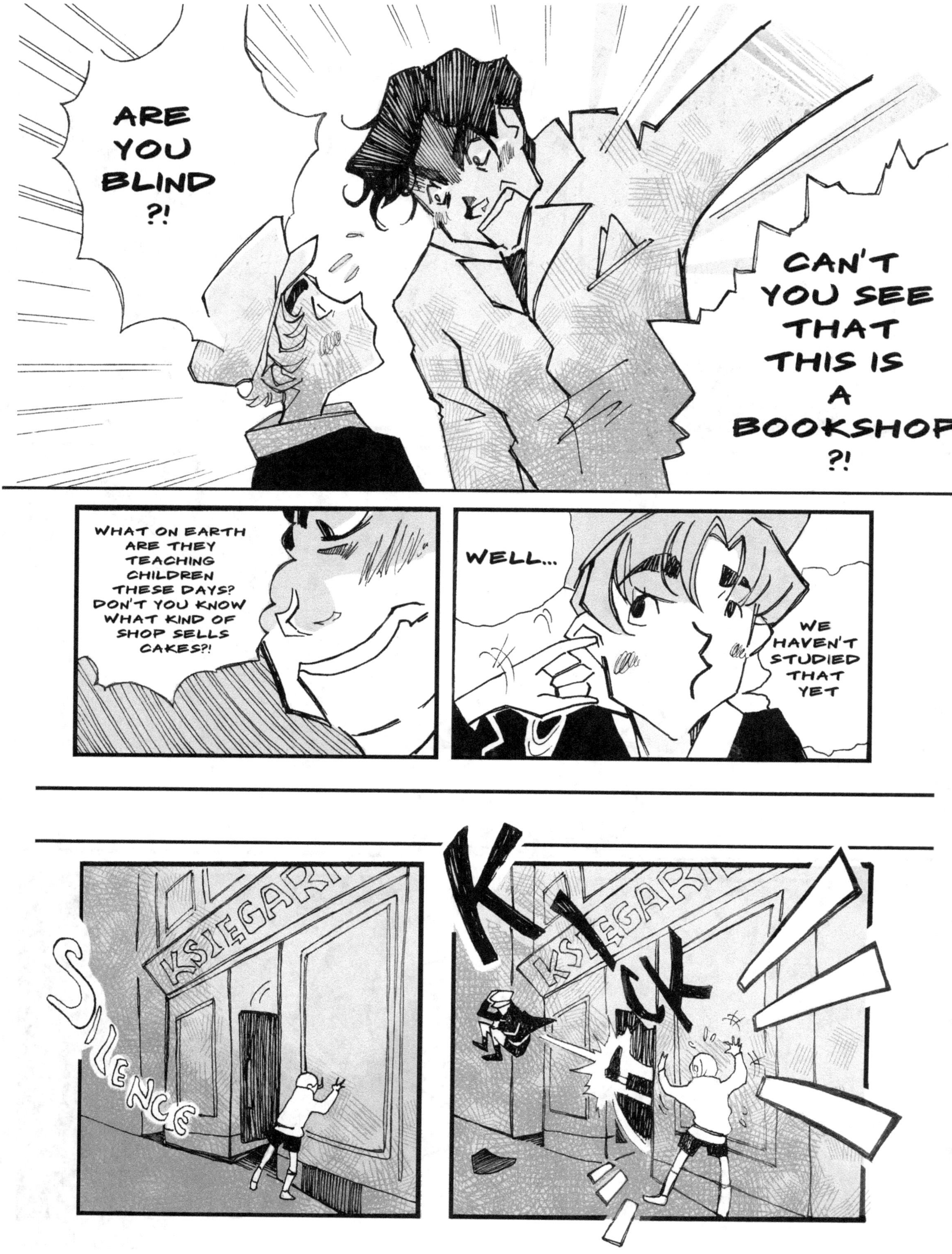

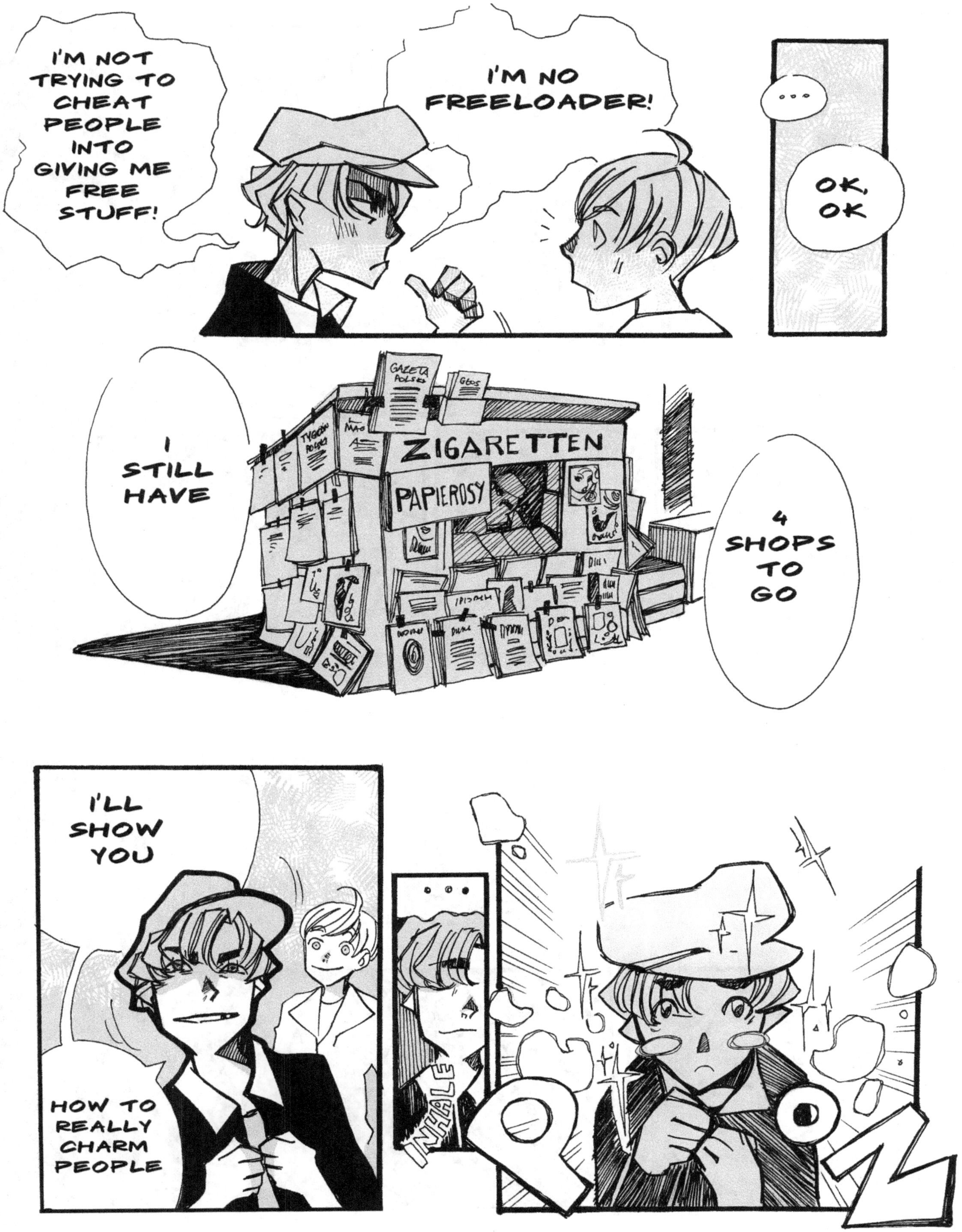

I'M NOT TRYING TO CHEAT PEOPLE INTO GIVING ME FREE STUFF!

I'M NO FREELOADER!

. . .

OK, OK

I STILL HAVE

ZIGARETTEN

PAPIEROSY

GAZETA POLSKA

GŁOS

4 SHOPS TO GO

I'LL SHOW YOU

HOW TO REALLY CHARM PEOPLE

INHALE

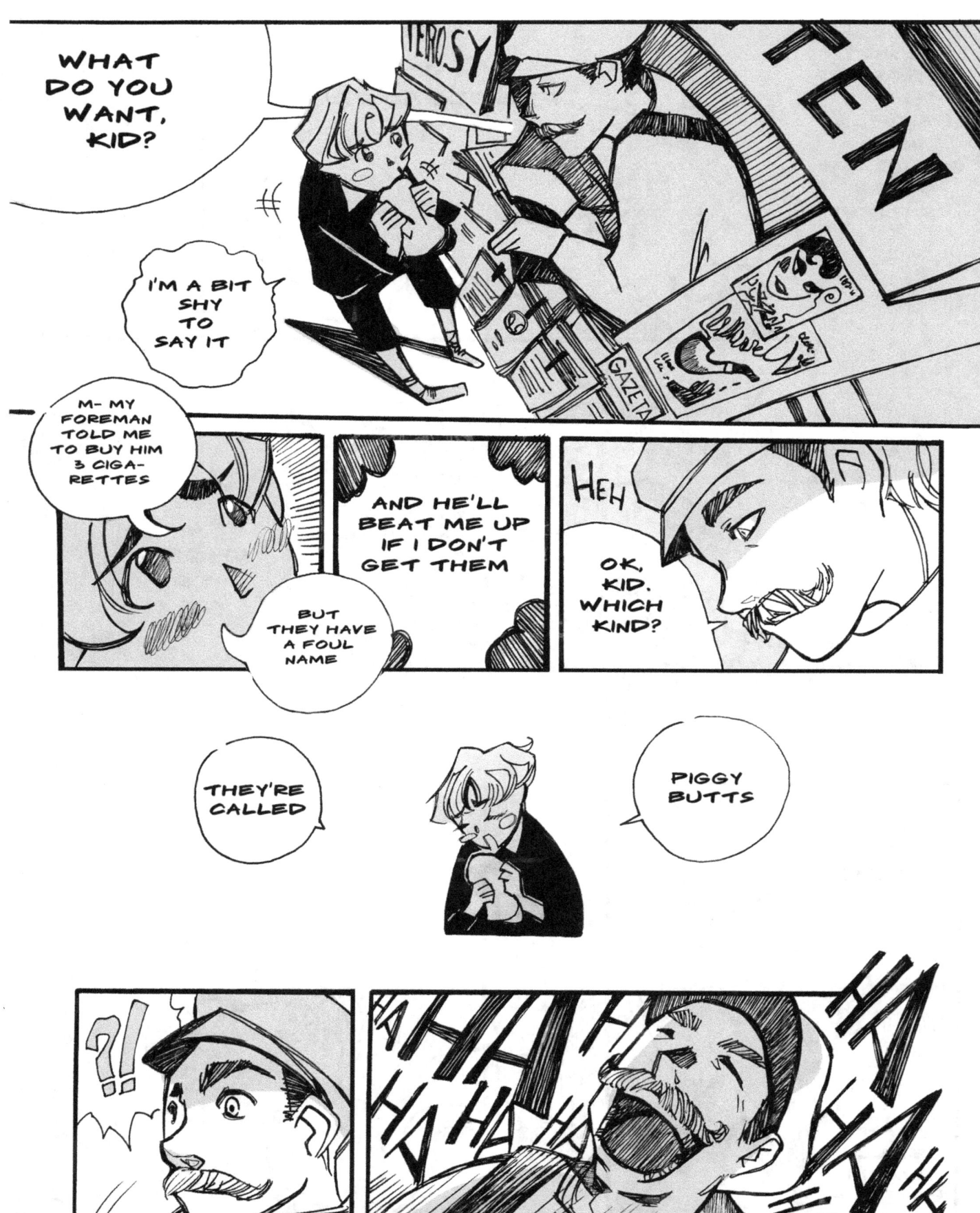

BUT I CAN DETECT ANY USE OF EVIL MAGIC, OR WHEN SOMEONE IS UNDER AN EVIL SPELL...

THE PEOPLE AROUND HIM KEPT CASTING EVIL SPELLS ON HIM

"YOU VERMIN"

"YOU PARASITE"

"YOU COCKROACH"

BUT HE DIDN'T KNOW ANY MAGIC

SO, HE COULDN'T DEFEND HIMSELF

... MY DAD MIGHT BE UNDER A SPELL TOO

I'M SORRY ...

WANNA GO PLAY IN THE PARK?

I CAN'T

MY MOTHER DOESN'T LET ME TALK TO STRANGERS, AND I CAN'T JUST LEAVE ...

WELL, WHAT'S YOUR NAME?

TOMEK

I'M ANTOS

SEE?

NOW WE'RE NOT STRANGERS ANYMORE!

TOMMY! DINNER'S READY!

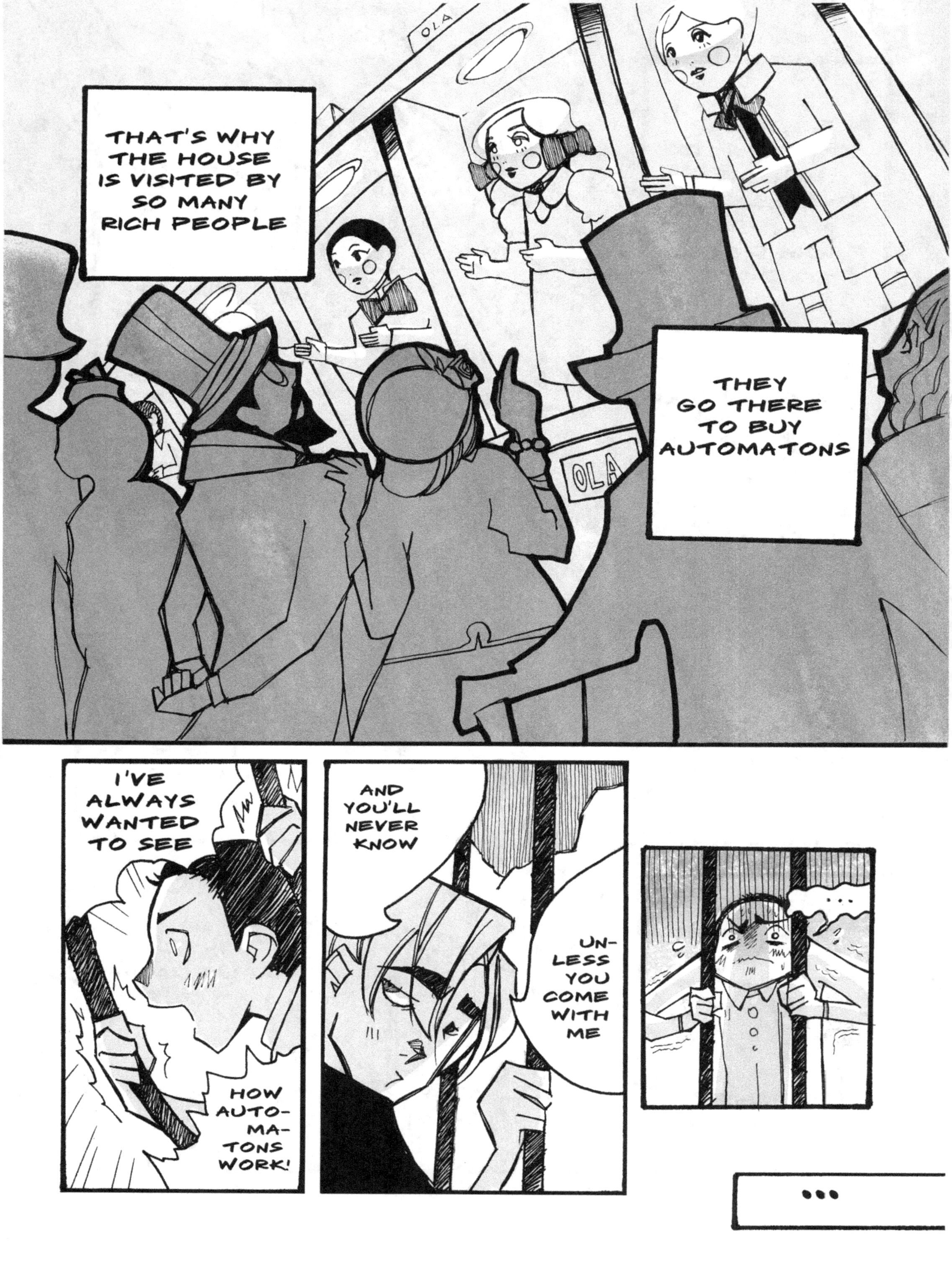

THAT'S WHY THE HOUSE IS VISITED BY SO MANY RICH PEOPLE

THEY GO THERE TO BUY AUTOMATONS

I'VE ALWAYS WANTED TO SEE

HOW AUTO-MA-TONS WORK!

AND YOU'LL NEVER KNOW

UN-LESS YOU COME WITH ME

...

...

...

WE'RE HERE

THEY'RE ALL AUTOMATONS?!

HOW DO THEY WORK?

IT'S SIMPLE: THEY WIND THEM UP

BUT HOW?

TEE HEE

TOMEK!

OH TOMEK!

DADDY HAD TO BE TAKEN

TO A SPECIAL HOSPITAL

...

NEXT DAY

UAAA

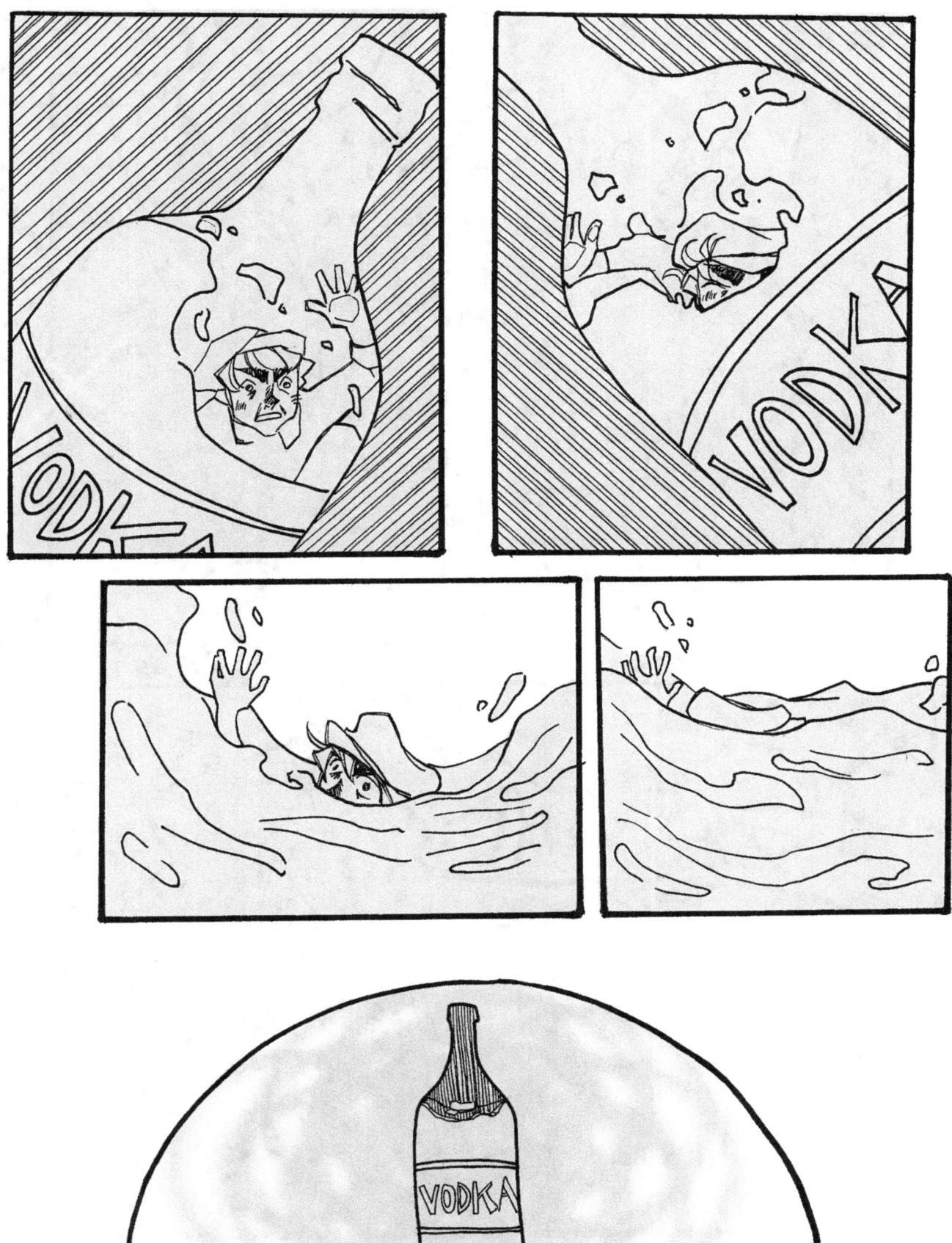

chapter II

A MONTH LATER

DOCTOR, PLEASE CONSIDER MY REQUEST TO ADMIT JÓZIA TO YOUR ORPHANAGE

SHE WILL HAVE MUCH BETTER CARE THERE, UNLIKE HERE

WE HAVE SO LITTLE SPACE, WE NEED MORE COAL AND MORE...

...

flick flick

HEHEHEHEHE

SIR!

PLEASE...
I KNOW YOU
TAKE
NO MONEY,
BUT...

TAKE
JOZIA

TO YOUR
ORPHA-
NAGE

K-SHANK

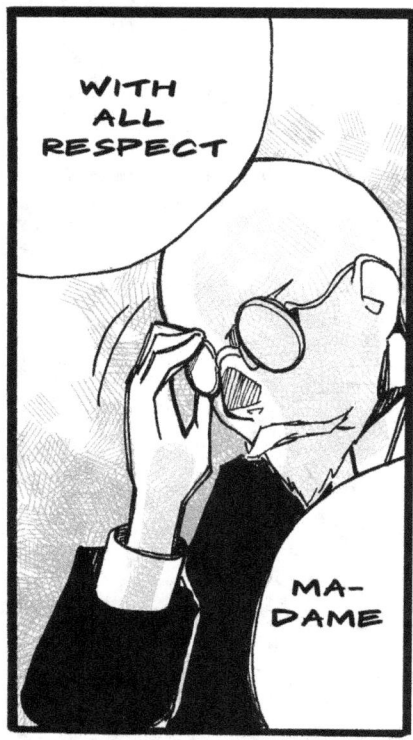

WITH
ALL
RESPECT

MA-
DAME

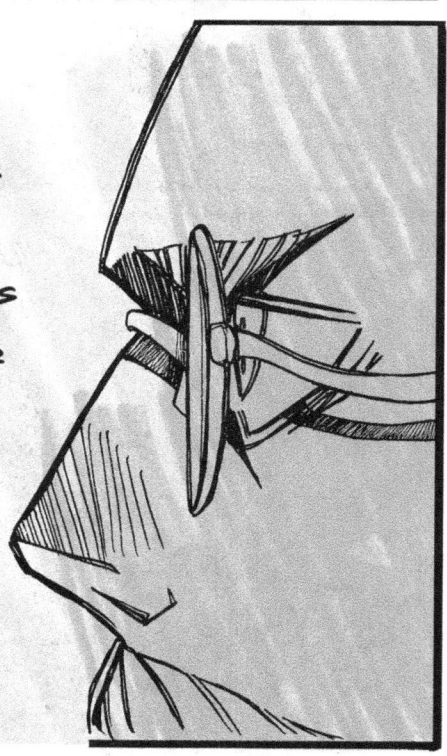

ARE YOU
AWARE
HOW MANY
APPLICATIONS
WE PROCESS
EVERY DAY?

FROM FAMILIES
THAT HAVE
NO ROOF OVER
THEIR HEADS,
WHO HAVE
NO FOOD FOR
THEIR
CHILDREN

2 HOURS LATER

MY CONDO-LENCES

ON YOUR HUS-BAND'S PASSING

I'M SURE YOUR APPLICATION WILL BE ACCEPTED

PLEASE BRING YOUR SON TO THE ORPHANAGE IN TWO WEEKS

GOD BLESS YOU, SIR

THAT EVENING...

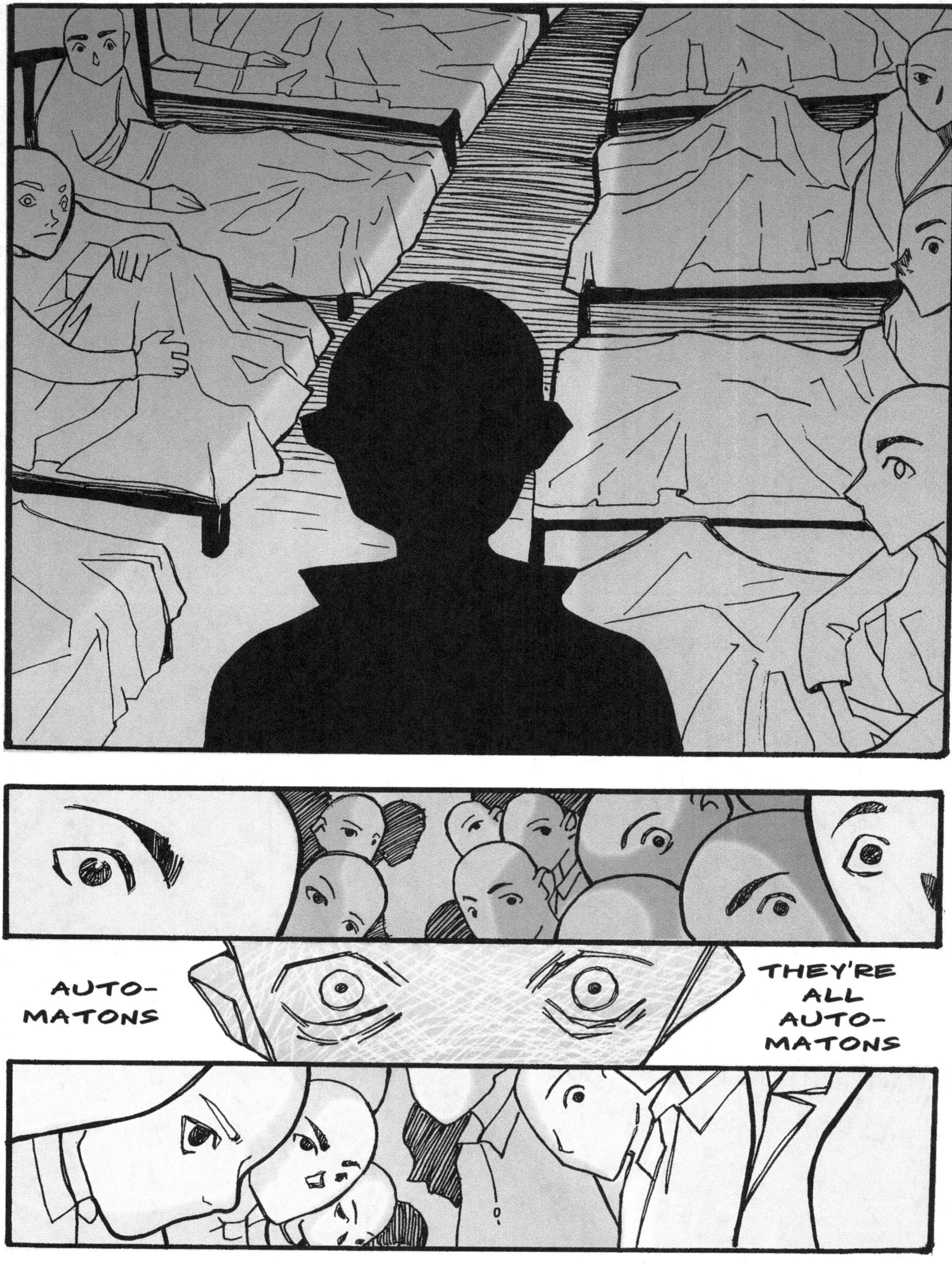

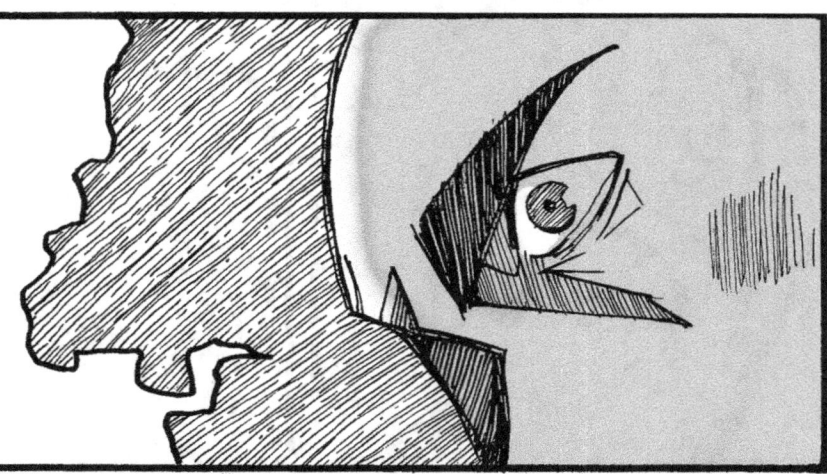

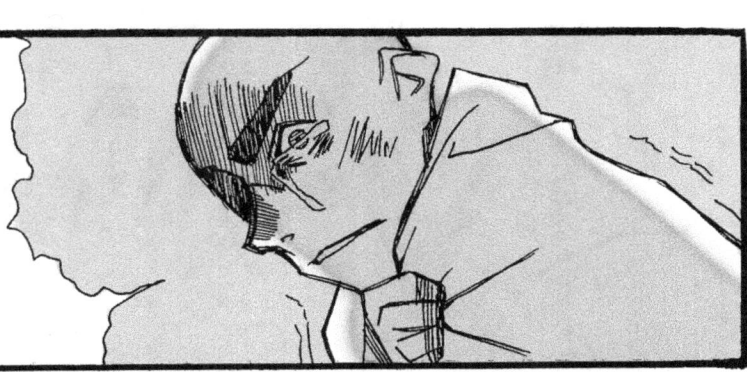

BUT I WON'T LET YOU TURN ME INTO ONE OF YOUR AUTOMATONS!

I HAVE TO DISSAPOINT YOU, KAJTEK

THIS HOME WAS CREATED TO MAKE SURE

THAT NO CHILD WOULD EVER BECOME AN AUTO-MATON

I BELIEVE THAT EVERY CHILD IS SPECIAL, AND THAT THEY SHOULD BE TREATED WITH RESPECT

...

WOOSH
I ALMOST BELIEVED YOU, OLD MAN !!!
IF THAT'S NOT AN AUTOMATON, THEN WHAT IS?!

chapter III

MY

CAP

LEAVE HER ALONE!

SHE'S JUST ON HER WAY TO SCHOOL.

WE DON'T WANT ANY TROUB...

I GO TO SCHOOL 'CAUSE I DON'T WANT TO END UP DUMB LIKE YOU!

SHUT UP!

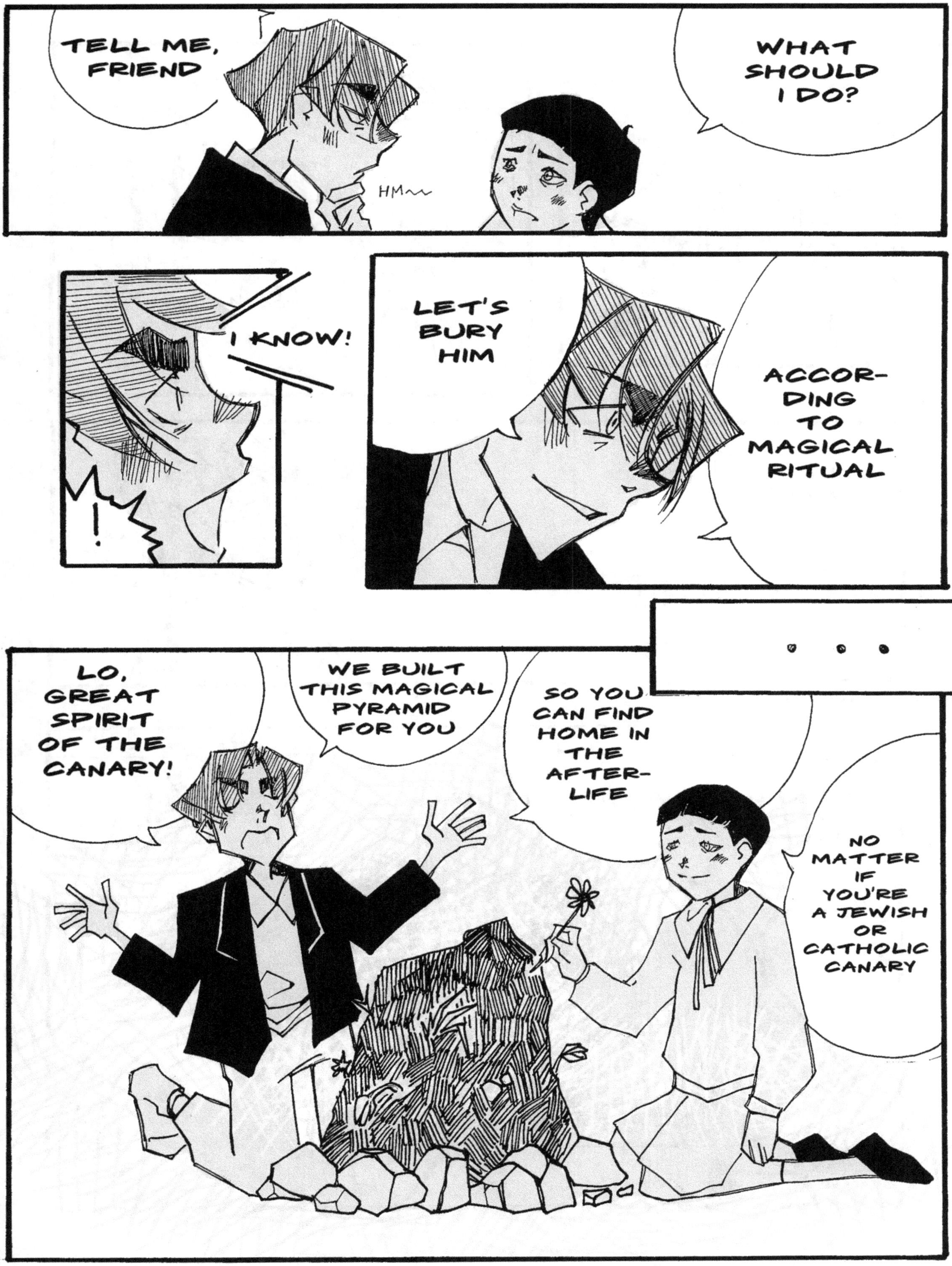

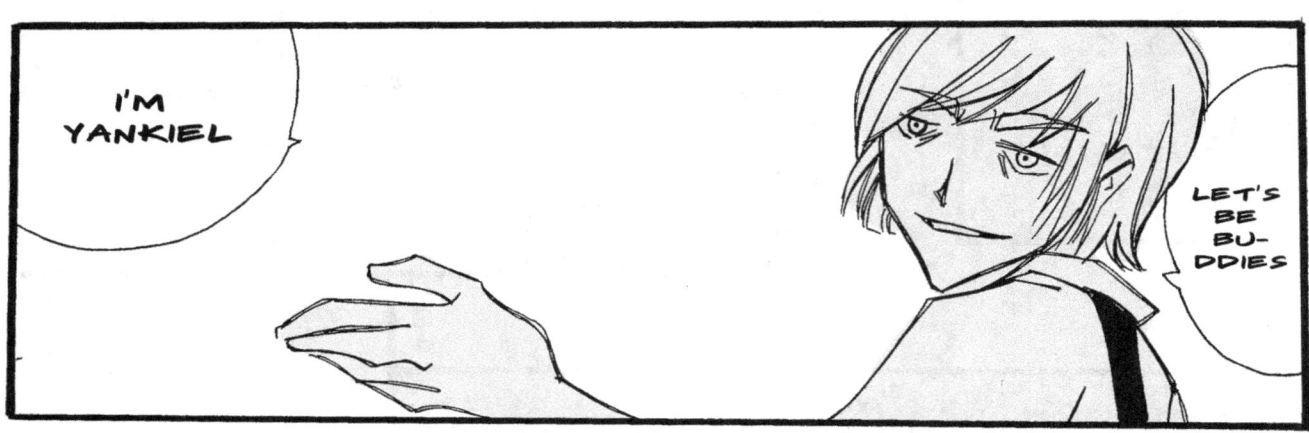

chapter IV

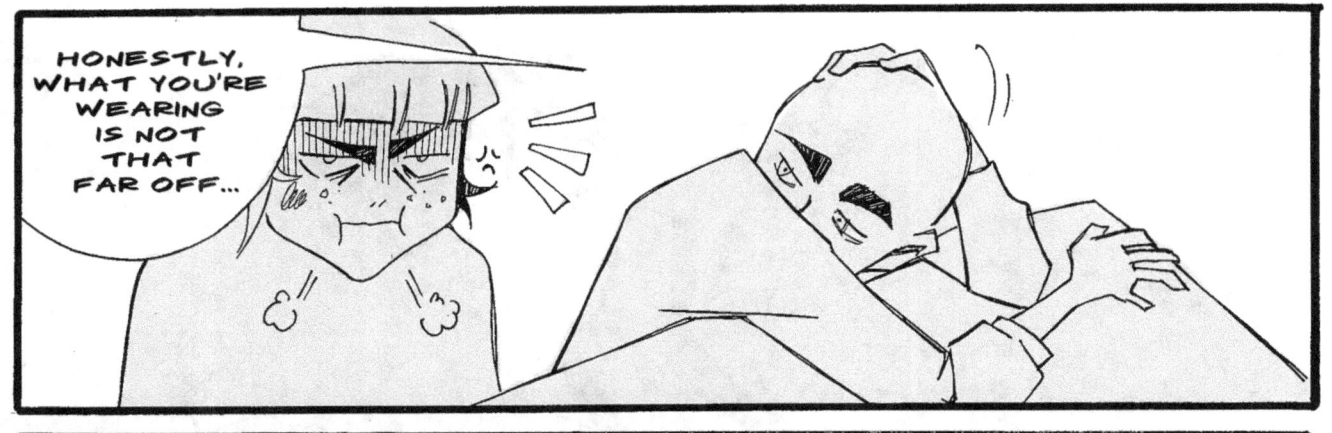

HONESTLY, WHAT YOU'RE WEARING IS NOT THAT FAR OFF...

YOU UNDER-STAND NOTHING!

MR. DOCTOR IS AGAINST UNIFORMS! HE SAYS EVERY CHILD IS DIFFERENT, SO WE SHOULDN'T HAVE TO ALL WEAR THE SAME CLOTHES. AND THAT'S NOT ALL.

KIDS HERE CAN DECIDE

IF THEY NEED TIME FOR THEM-SELVES

THEY CAN GO TO THE "QUIET ROOM"

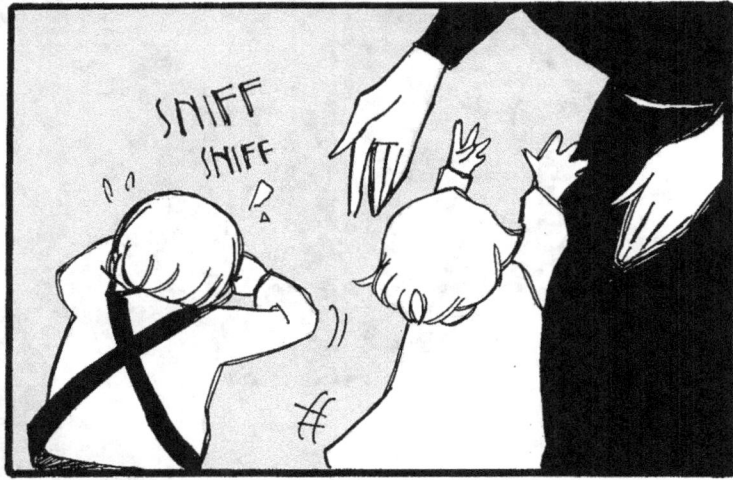

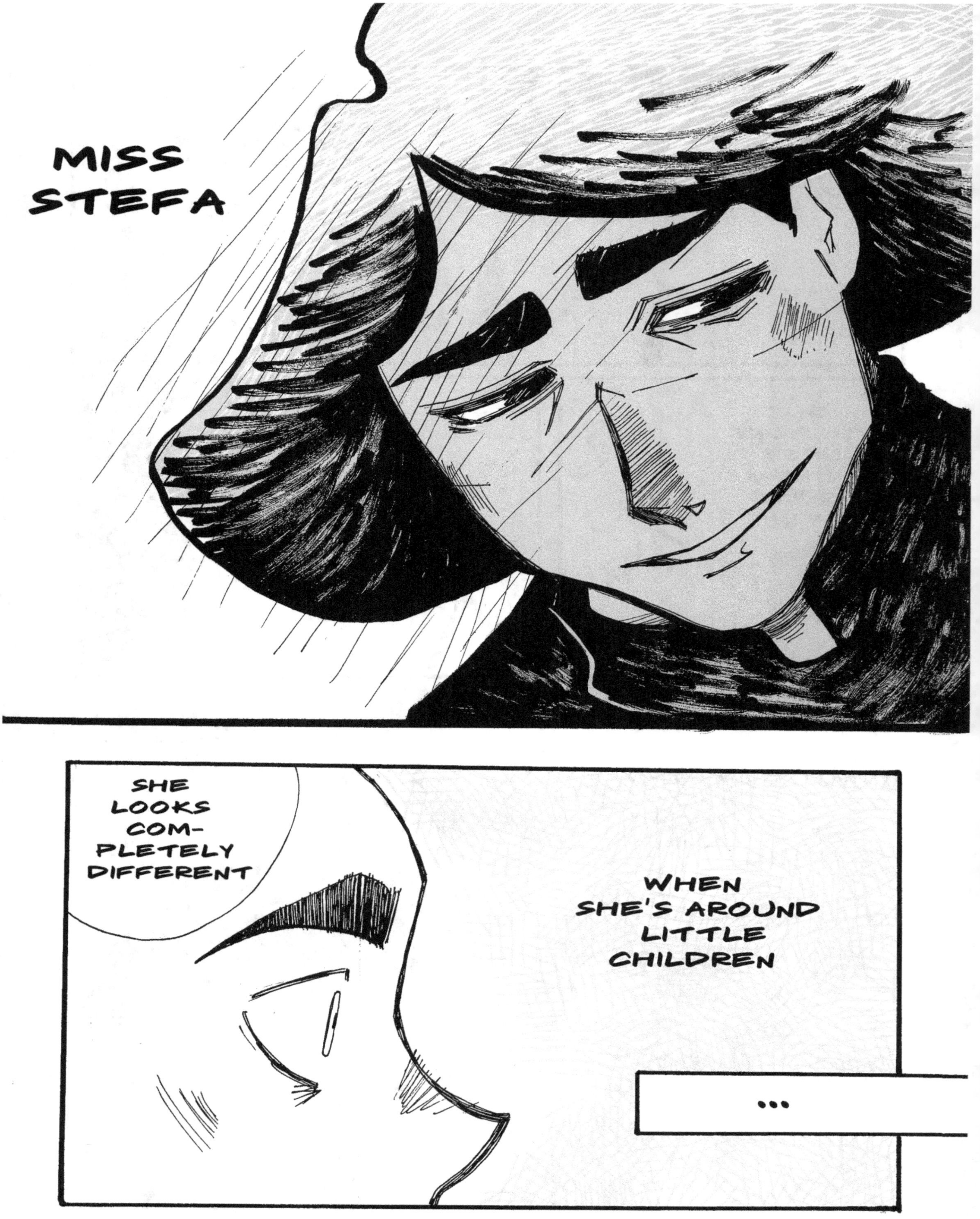

MISS
STEFA

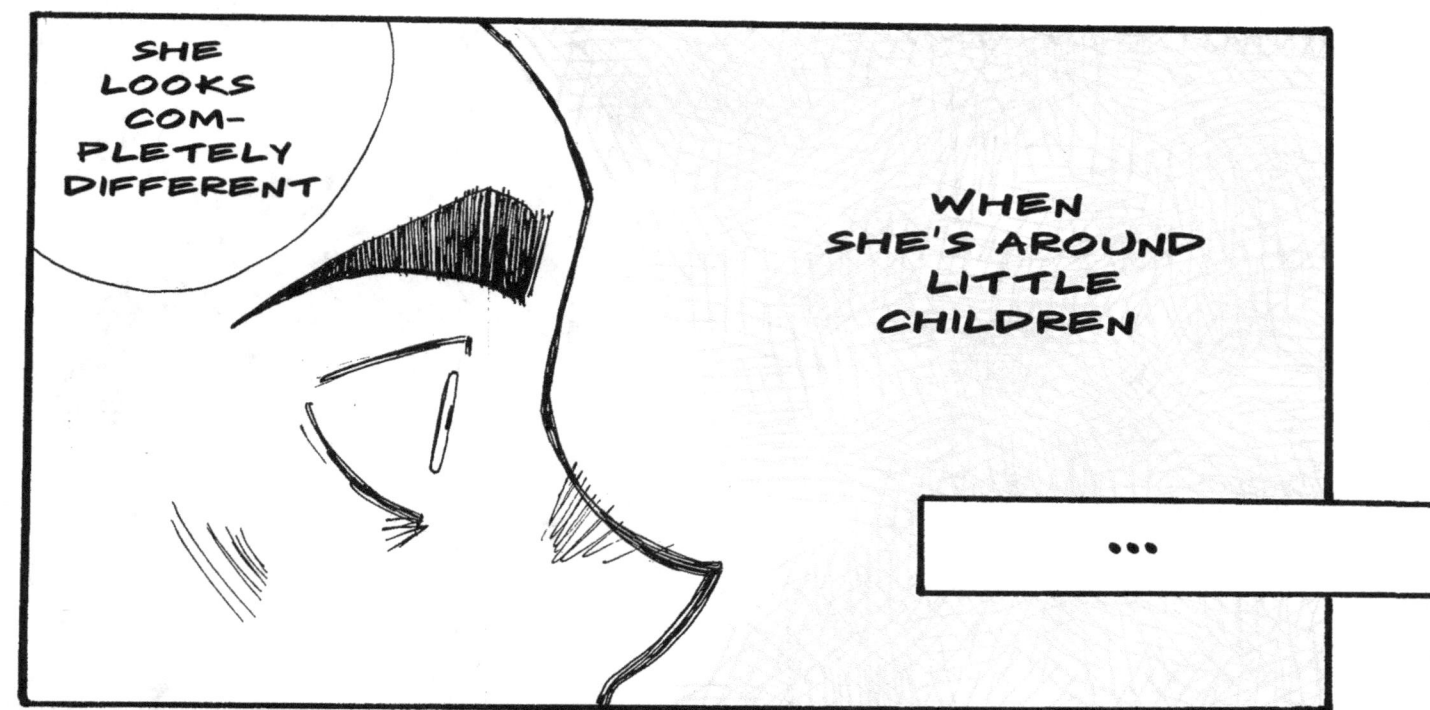

chapter
V

NOW, LET'S PROCEED TO THE CASE OF HELCIA

WHO SKIPPED A CLASS

...

HELCIU, YOUR PUNISH-MENT WILL BE

TO TAKE AWAY YOUR WEEKLY DUTY

OF HELPING MALCOLM WITH HIS HOMEWORK

NO OBJEC-TION

sniff

YOUR HONOUR

?!

?!

NICE PUNISHMENT! NO KNEELING ON GRAVEL...

AND YOU DON'T HAVE TO DO ANYTHING FOR A WEEK! LUCKY!

YOU KNOW NOTHING, SILLY!

I'LL HAVE NOTHING TO DO FOR A WHOLE WEEK. LIKE SOME PATHETIC PRINCESS.

LET'S MOVE ON TO KAJTEK'S CASE

BARUCH WILL TAKE THE PUNISHMENT, AS HE'S THE MENTOR RESPONSIBLE.

BARUCH, YOU HAVE TO TALK TO KAJTEK EVERY DAY TO AQUAINT HIM BETTER WITH OUR HOME'S REGULATIONS

THIS MEANS THAT, ACCORDING TO ARTICLE 1000,

YOU WILL HAVE TO LEAVE THE CHILDREN'S HOME

ARE THERE ANY OBJECTIONS ?

chapter
VI

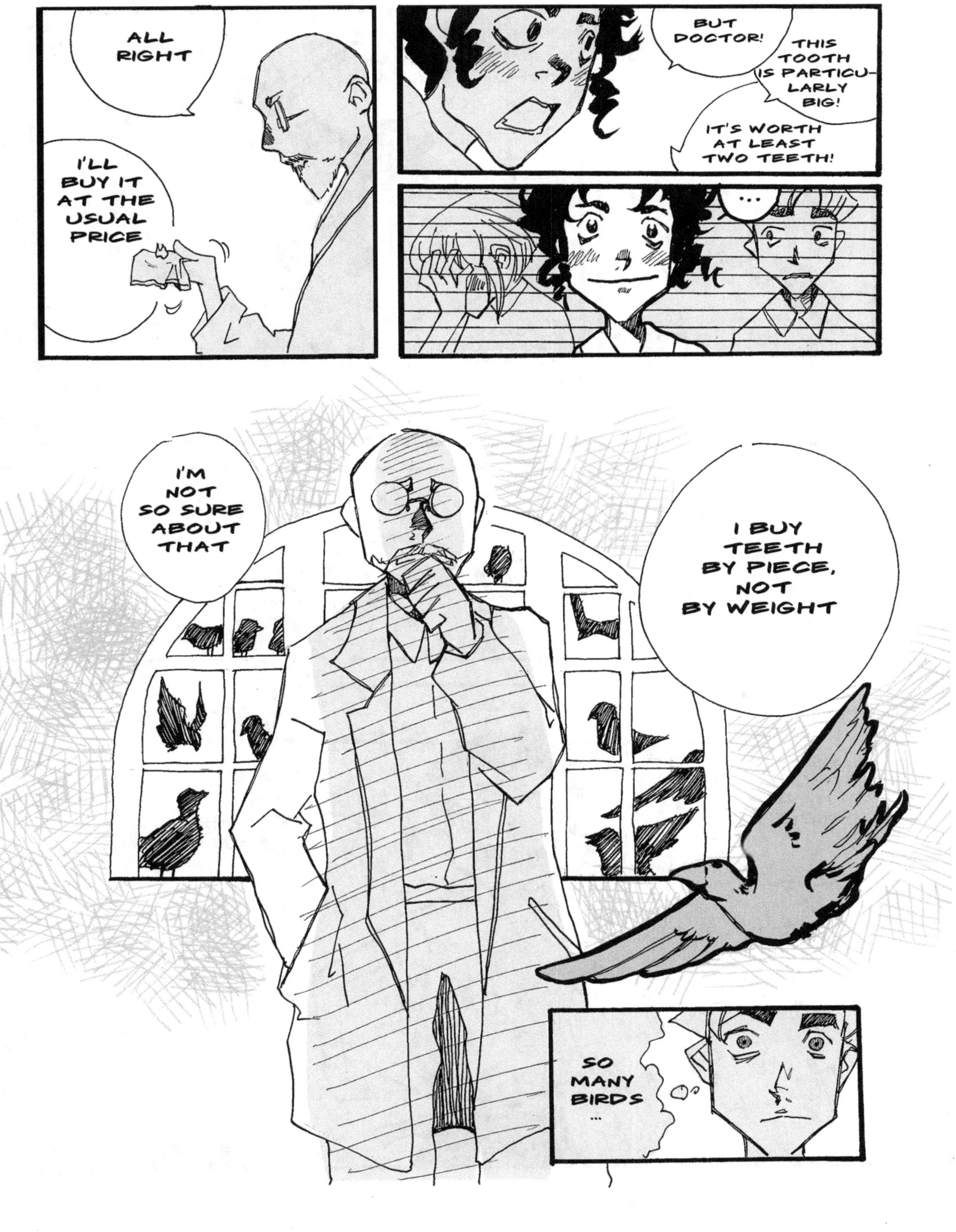

BOM
SHOE POLISH!
GET YER SHOE POLISH! RIGHT HERE!
HEY! WATCH WHERE YOU'RE GOING, KID!
SHOE POLISH!
GOING FAST!
IT'S YAN-KIEL!
YANKIEL? HEY!
HOW'S IT GOING?

...
...
DOCTOR
WASN'T YANKIEL RIGHT?
IN OUR CHILDREN'S HOME WE LEARN ABOUT RESPECT AND HELPING EACH OTHER
BUT EVEN ADULTS DON'T FOLLOW THESE VALUES
WHAT'S THE USE OF IT THEN?
HM...
UPON LEAVING THIS HOUSE EVERYONE SHOULD HAVE THE MAGICAL SKILL
MA GICAL?!
OF COUNTING TO FIVE

HE APPROACHED THE PRINCE
AND ASKED:
YOUNG MAN DO YOU KNOW
HAPPINESS?
YES
THAT'S ONE.
DO YOU KNOW FEAR?
YES
THAT'S TWO
DO YOU KNOW KINDNESS?
YES
THAT'S THREE
DO YOU KNOW GRATITUDE?
YES
THAT'S FOUR
DO YOU KNOW HUMILITY?
YES
THAT'S FIVE

chapter VII

...
OUT OF MY WAY LOSERS!
DASH
WHERE'S HE RUSHING TO?
DON'T YOU KNOW WHAT DAY IT IS TODAY?
TODAY IS A BETTING DAY!

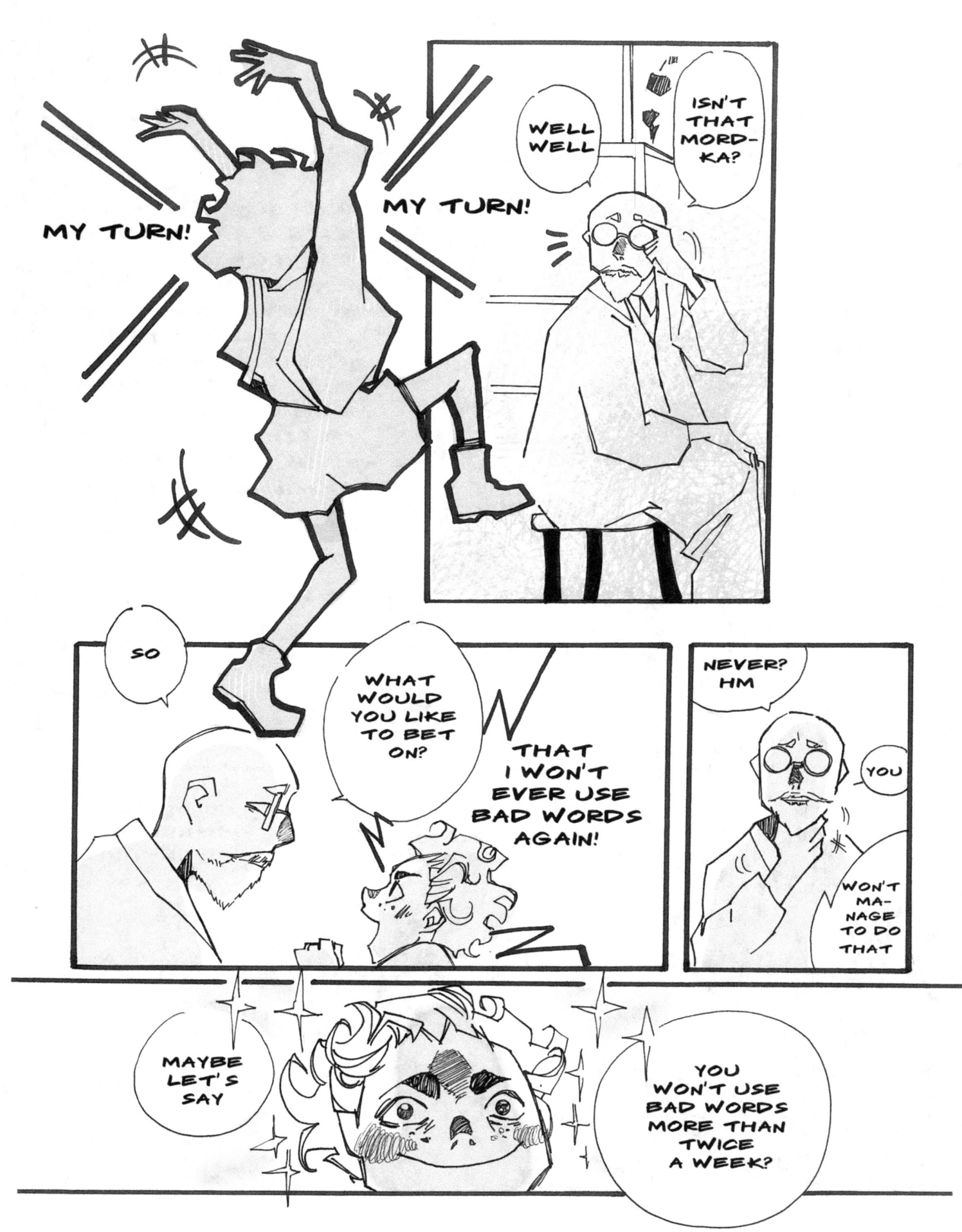

ARE YOU SURE

WE'RE ALLOWED IN HERE?

YES

ARE THESE THE CANDIES YOU WON?

YES

IS THAT SOME KIND OF A FAD? I SAW OTHER CHILDREN ALSO PUTTING THEM AWAY IN SMALL BOXES

NO, SILLY

I'M KEEPING THESE

SNAP

FOR MY LITTLE COUSIN

SOME CHILDREN STASH THE CANDIES AWAY FOR THE WEEKEND SO, WHEN THEY ARE VISITED BY THEIR RELATIVES THEY CAN HAVE A SWEET SURPRISE FOR THEM

THAT'S A NICE IDEA. THAT WE HAVE SOMETHING TO GIVE TO VISITORS FROM THE OUTSIDE.

Y'KNOW, TODAY I TALKED TO DANIEL...

HE'LL SOON HAVE TO LEAVE OUR HOUSE

HE'S TERRIFIED OF WHAT AWAITS HIM OUT THERE

AND I DON'T EVEN KNOW HOW TO CHEER HIM UP

I WAS SUPPOSED TO BE A GREAT SORCERER

I'M AFRAID THAT ONCE I LEAVE THIS HOUSE

I'LL BE TAKEN OVER BY THE MAGIC THAT TURNS PEOPLE INTO ROACHES

BUT JUST LIKE DANIEL

ROACHES?

WHAT ARE YOU TALKING ABOUT?

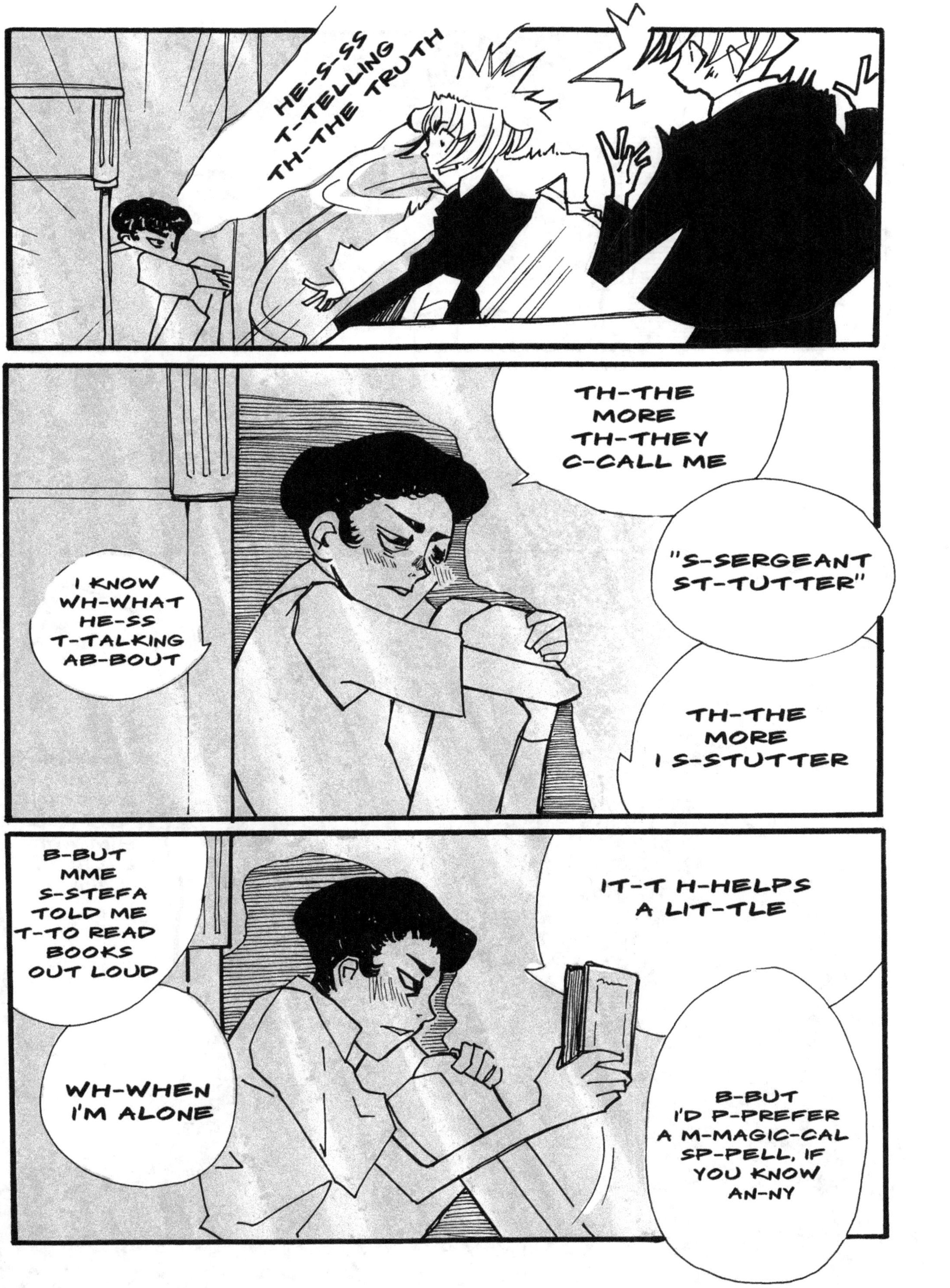

W-WE ALL GATHERED IN FR-FRONT OF TH-THE HOUSE
I W-WAS S-SCARED
M-MY GRANDP-PA W-WANTED TO M-MAKE P-PEACE
BUT
...
GRAB

chapter VIII

SPRING, 1940

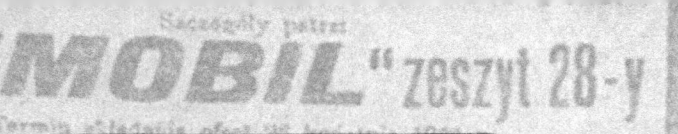

It is believed that Sister Faustyna used the miraculous power of bilocation to be in two places at the same time. Investigations are on-going..

SISTER FAUSTYNA WHO USED BILOCATION

SISTER FAUSTYNA WHO USED BILOCATION

BI

LOCATION

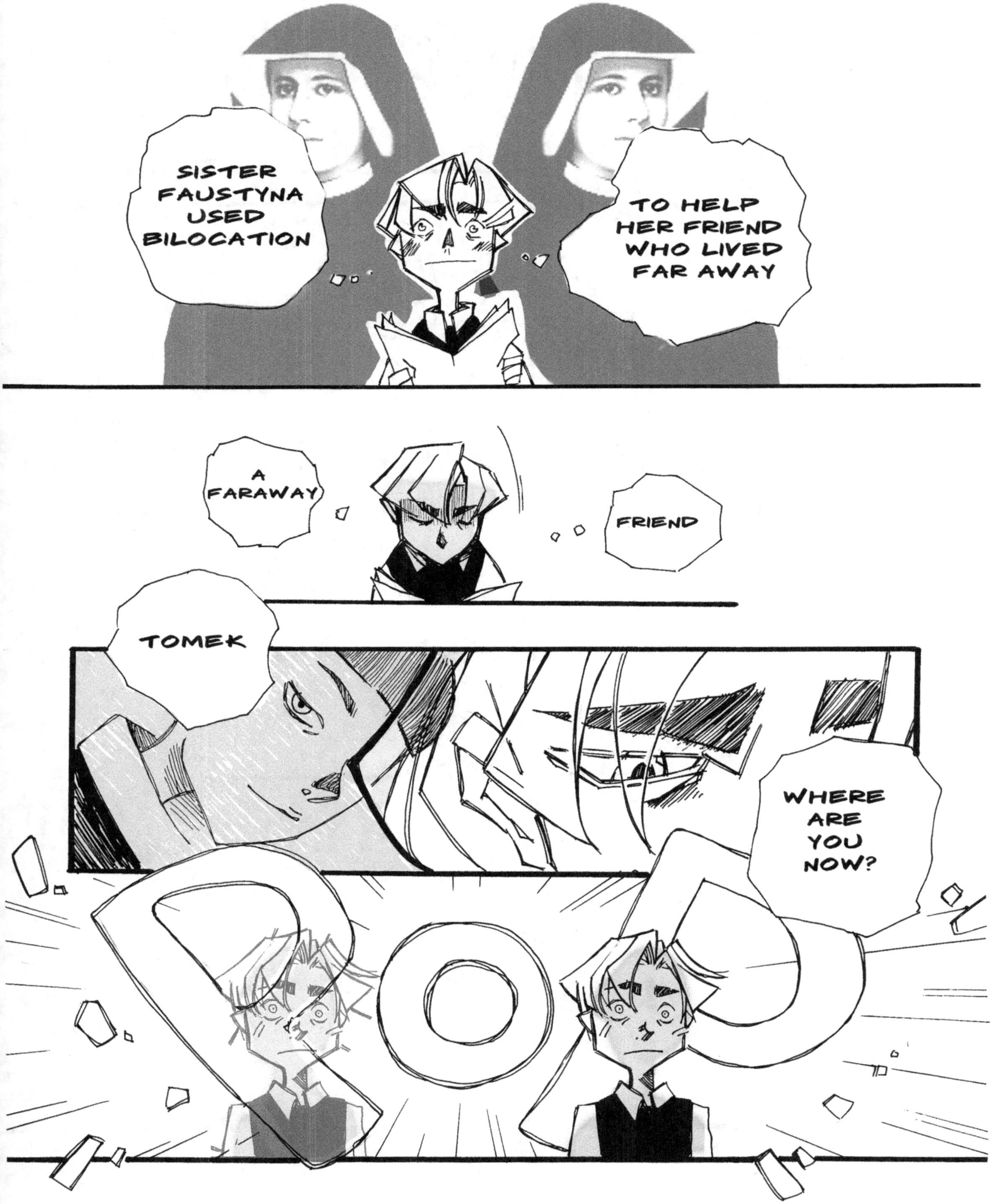
SISTER FAUSTYNA USED BILOCATION
TO HELP HER FRIEND WHO LIVED FAR AWAY
A FARAWAY
FRIEND
TOMEK
WHERE ARE YOU NOW?

I REGRET TO INFORM YOU THAT

DESPITE THE BEST EFFORTS BY OUR PSY-CHIATRIC WARD...

COVER YOUR EARS, TOMEK

YOUR HUSBAND COMMITED SUICIDE

TO--

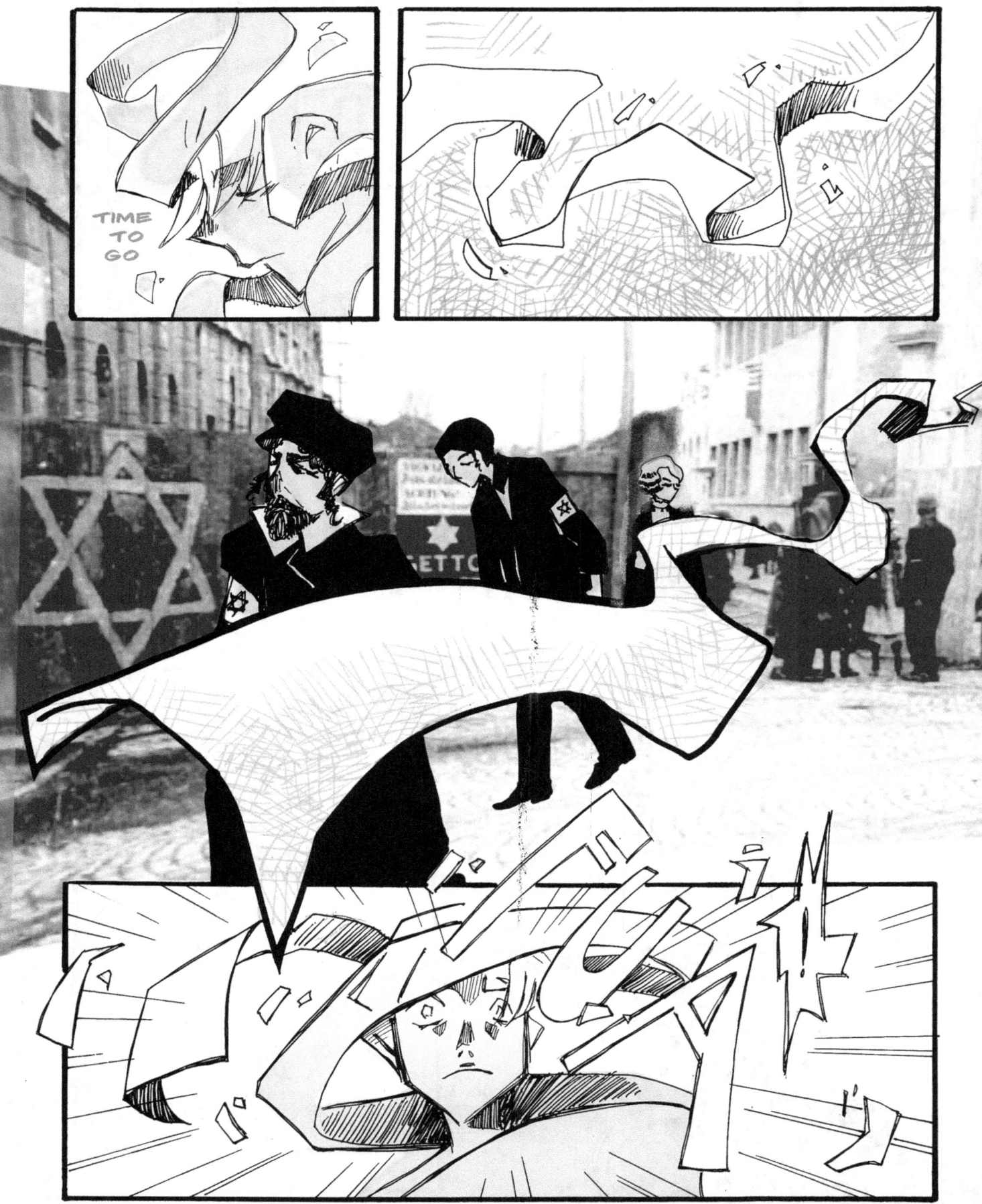

ARM-BAND?!*

AND WHERE'S YOUR

GRAB

THIS IS

BAD

*SINCE SEPTEMBER 1939
JEWS WERE FORCED TO WEAR
A BADGE WITH A STAR OF DAVID

I TOSSED IT

...

CLICK

COME WITH US

BEHIND THAT CORNER

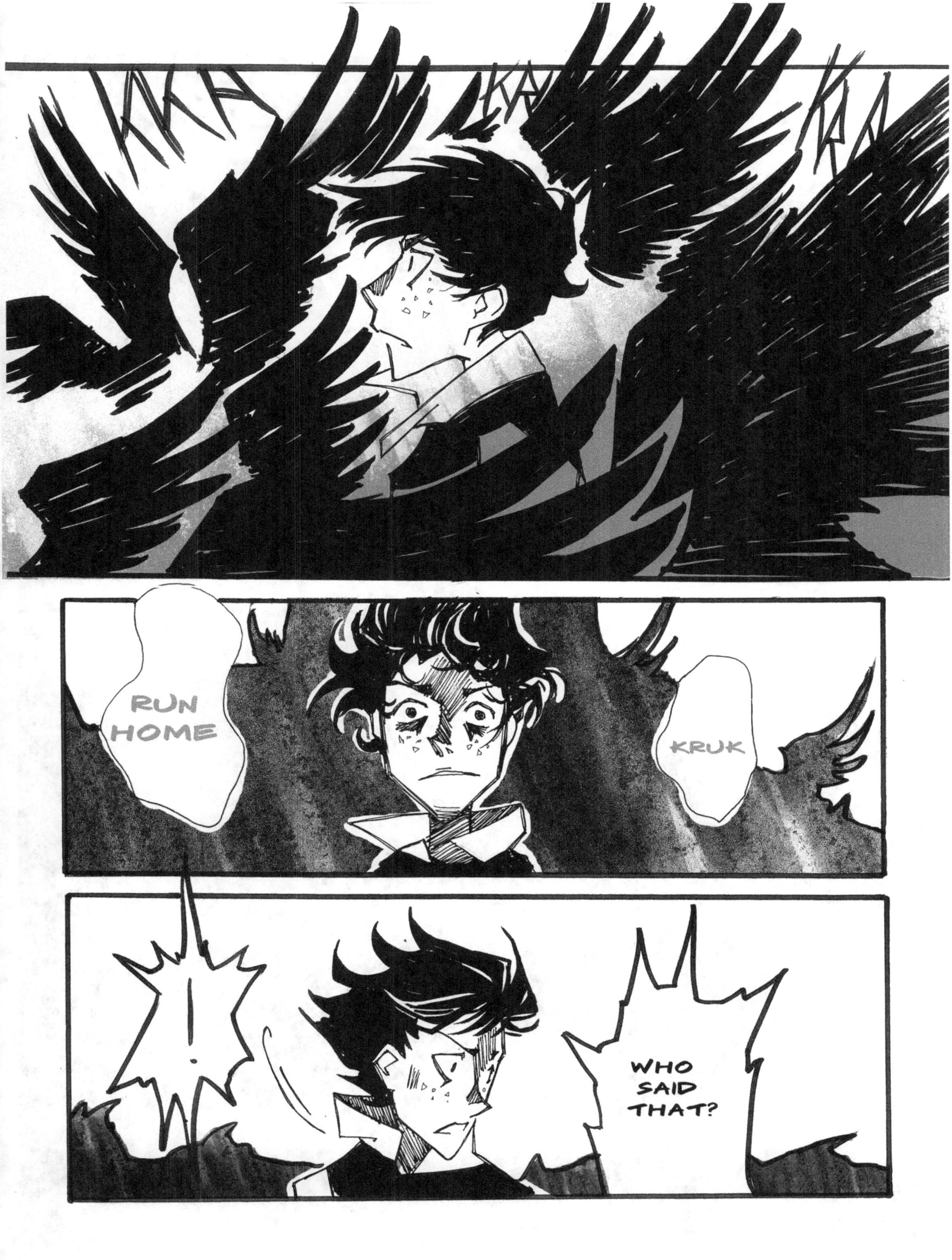

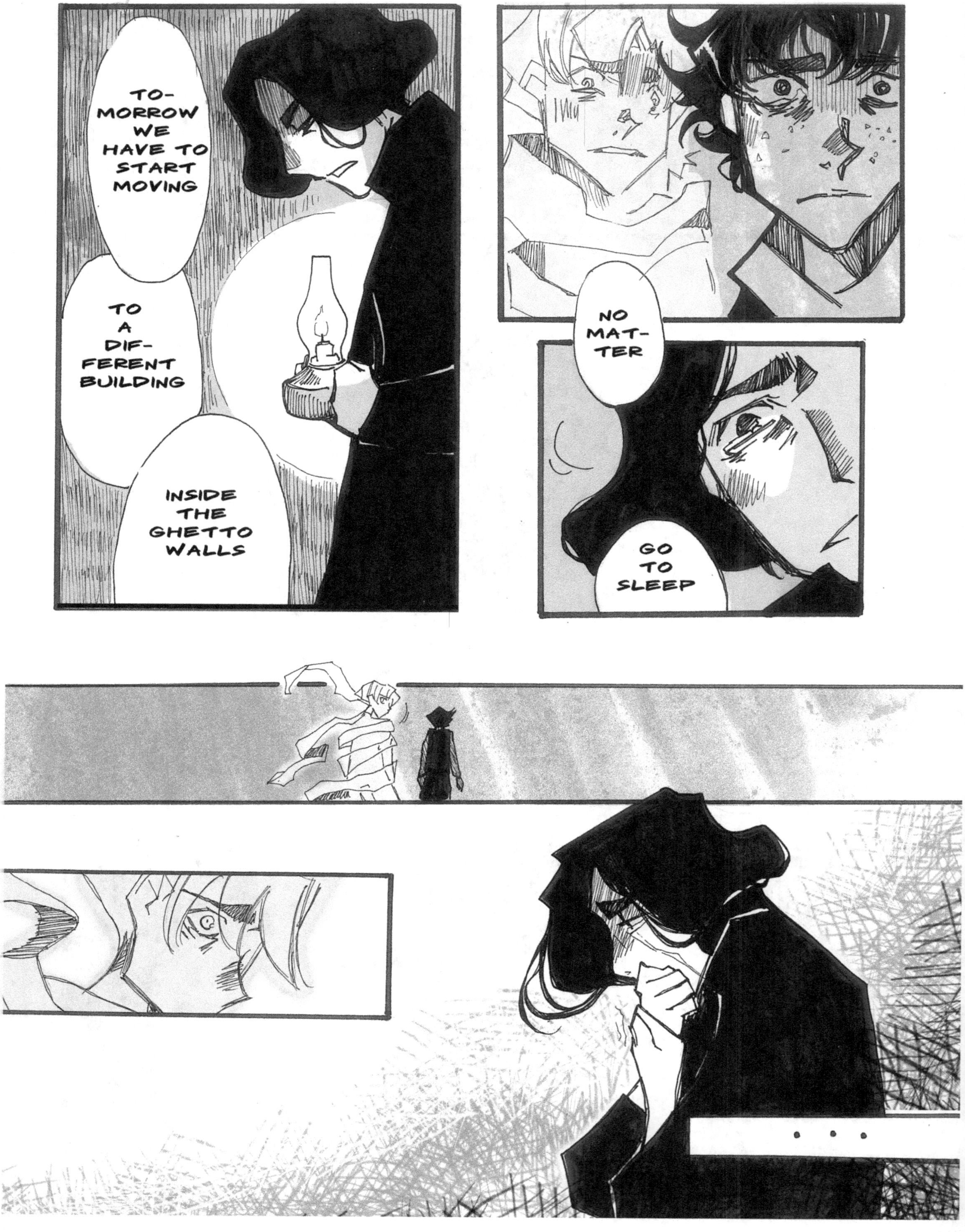

chapter IX

AFTER THE INVASION IN SEPTEMBER 1939, NAZI GERMANY
OCCUPIED THE WEST OF POLAND,
WHILE THE EAST WAS ANNEXED BY THE SOVIET UNION.
IN THEIR ATTEMPT TO ESCAPE PERSECUTION FROM THE NAZIS,
MANY INHABITANTS OF CENTRAL AND WESTERN POLAND
MOVED TO THE EASTERN BORDERLANDS. SOON, HOWEVER,
THESE FELL UNDER CONTROL OF THE SOVIET UNION,
WHOSE ARMY STARTED DEPORTATIONS OF POLISH
POPULATION TO OTHER AREAS OF THE U.S.S.R., SUCH AS SIBERIA.

IN 1940 THE GERMANS BEGAN REGULAR
ROUNDUPS (ŁAPANKI) OF CIVILIANS.
THESE PEOPLE WERE CHOSEN MOSTLY AT RANDOM,
AND MAJORITY OF THEM WERE ARRESTED, TAKEN
TO LABOR CAMPS, OR EXECUTED.
IT WAS THE TIME OF LIFE-DEFINING DECISIONS FOR MANY.
IN THE MIDST OF MASSIVE RELOCATIONS OF POPULATIONS,
FAMILIES WERE TO BE SEPARATED, SOME NEVER TO MEET AGAIN.

ARE YOU SURE ABOUT IT, NATHAN?

HELCIA WILL BE SAFER HERE

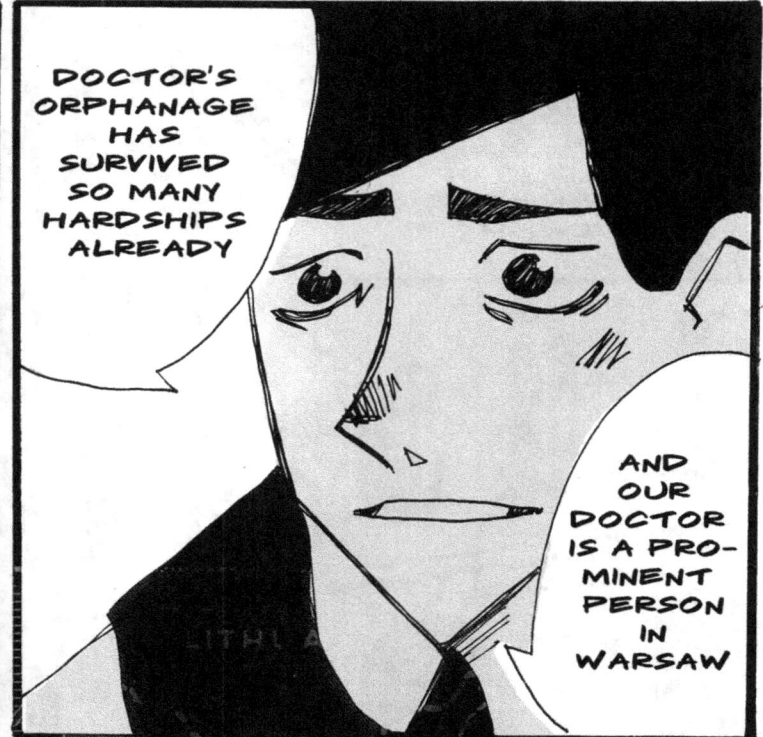

DOCTOR'S ORPHANAGE HAS SURVIVED SO MANY HARDSHIPS ALREADY

AND OUR DOCTOR IS A PRO-MINENT PERSON IN WARSAW

HE'S GOT A BROAD BACK, TOO

NO-ONE WILL DARE TO HURT US

WE HAVE SUPPORTERS AMONG IMPORTANT PEOPLE, WHO WONT'T LET--

HELCIA ...

KAJTEK!

YOU HAVE TO TEACH ME MAGIC!

SHUSH!

IT'S A SECRET!

WE'LL DEFEND THE ORPHA-NAGE TOGE-THER!

WITH MAGIC!

DO YOU UNDERSTAND?!

SHAKE SHAKE

OH!

THAT'S THE NEW BOY

I'VE HEARD HIS DAD WENT BANK-RUPT

AND HIS MOTHER DIED OF TYPHUS

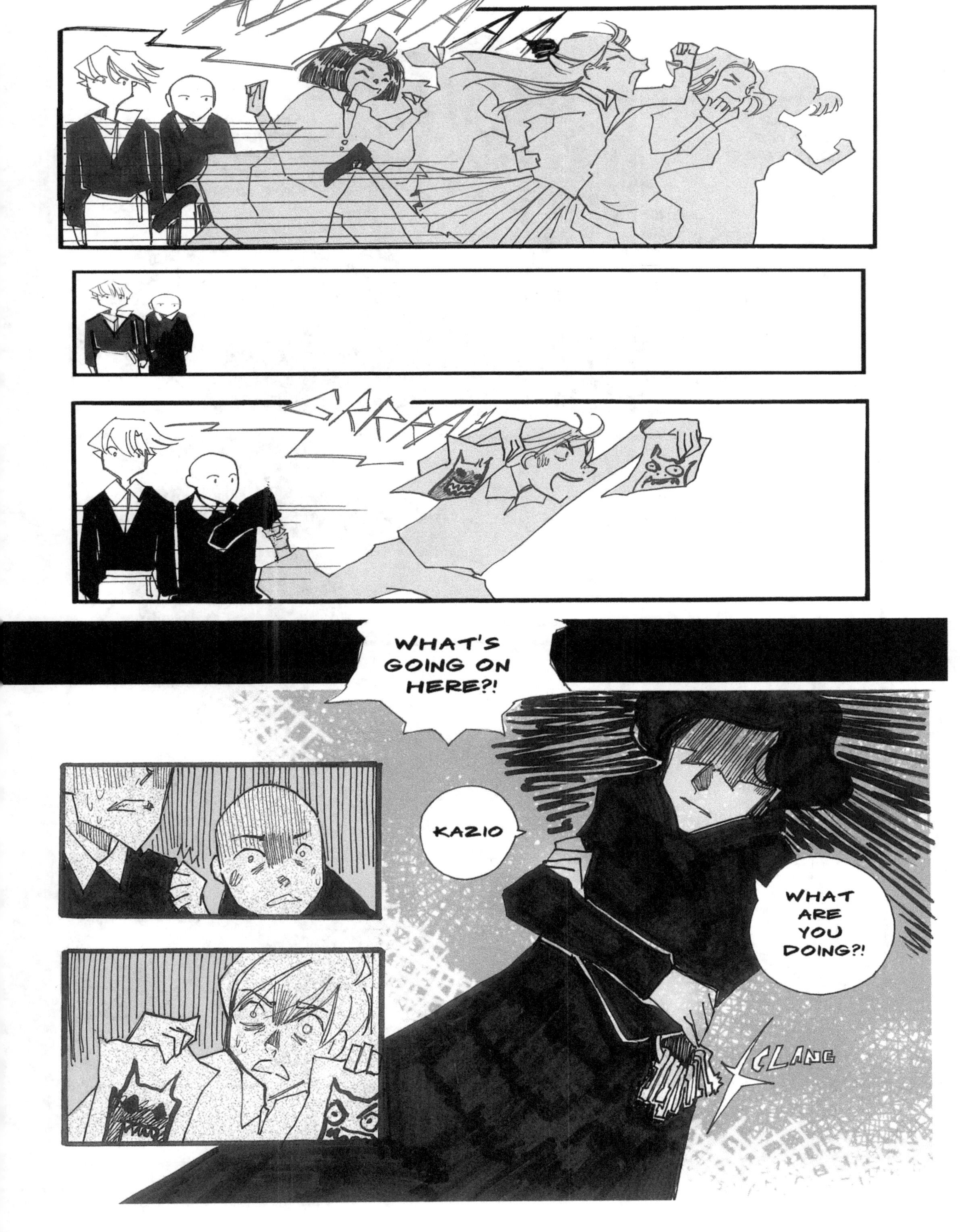

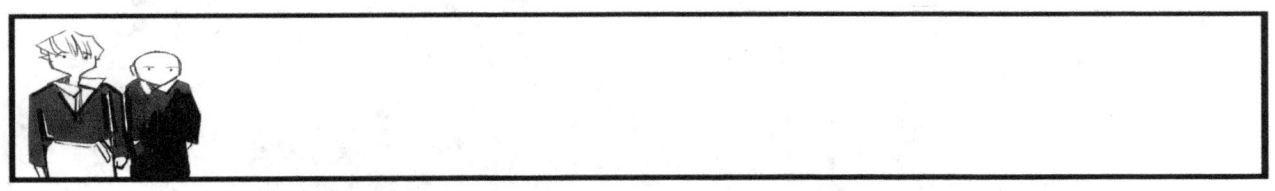

WHAT'S GOING ON HERE?!

KAZIO

WHAT ARE YOU DOING?!

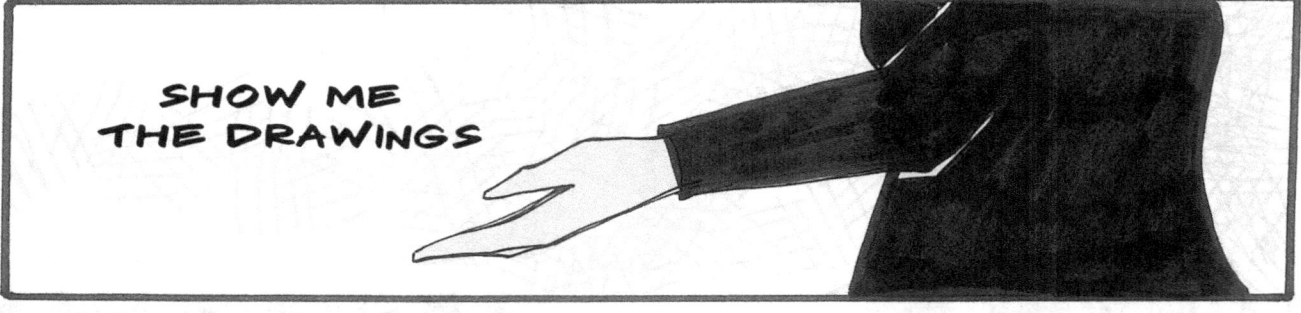

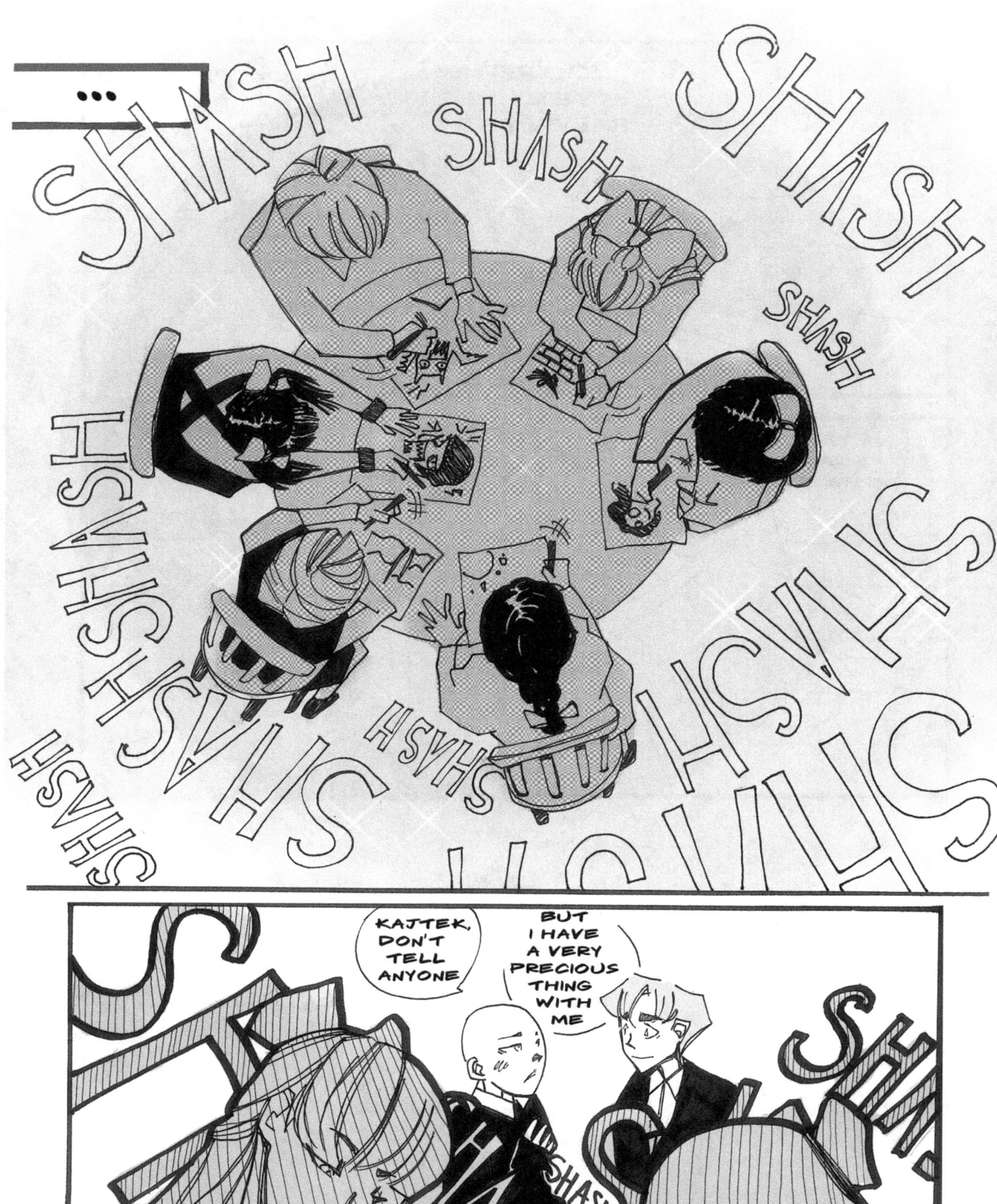

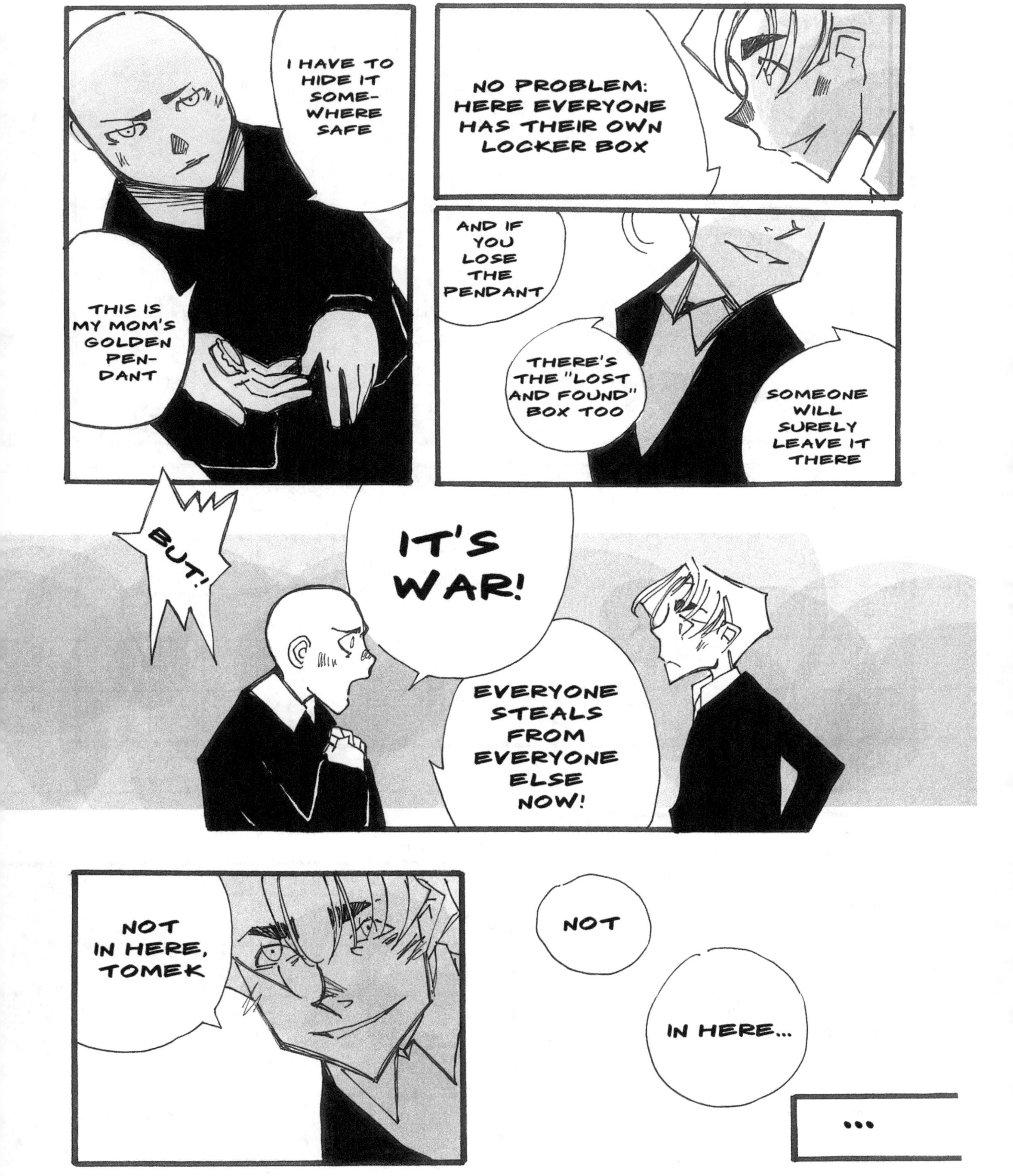

chapter
X

SARA SEEMS TO BE SADDER THAN ISMAEL

ALTHOUGH SHE GOT NEUTRAL VOTES

Sniffle

TRUE

BUT A NEUTRAL RESULT MEANS THAT YOU DON'T ENGAGE IN HOUSE ACTIVITIES, AND NONE OF THE CHILDREN KNOW WHO YOU ARE.

SOME CHILDREN WOULD PREFER NEGATIVE VOTES

TO VOTES THAT SHOW NO ONE CARES ABOUT YOU

ISMAEL, WE KEEP GETTING COMPLAINTS ABOUT YOU, AND YET YOU NEVER TRY TO IMPROVE. RECENTLY YOU KICKED OLA, AND YOU WERE TOLD TO WRITE HER A LETTER OF APOLOGY, BUT YOU DIDN'T.

IF NOBODY VOUCHES FOR YOU CORRECTING YOUR BEHAVIOR

YOU'LL HAVE TO LEAVE THIS HOUSE

BUT HE'S A GOOD PERSON, SO IF HE DOES SOME-THING BAD AGAIN
I'LL TAKE THE PUNISH-MENT FOR HIM
DO YOU ALL AGREE TO
SUCH CONDITIONS?
YES!
YES!
YES!
YES!

ISMAEL, ALL ARE IN FAVOUR,

SO YOU CAN GO BACK TO YOUR SEAT

MISS STICK-UP-HER-BUM

I HAVE ONE REQUEST

CAN I GET SOME PAPER AND A PENCIL?

WRITE THAT APOLOGY LETTER

I'D LIKE TO

IF YOU'D LIKE

WE CAN HELP YOU WRITE IT

NO NEED

...

UH

HOW SHOULD I START?

START WITH "DEAR OLA..."

AND WRITE HOW YOU FEEL

DON'T PEEK!

IL VA SE NOYER DANS TOUTE CETTE GENTILLESSE

WRITE THAT YOU'RE SORRY

AND YOU WON'T DO IT AGAIN

YOU CAN ALSO ADD THAT AND

AND--

TEE HEE!

SCRIBBLE SCRIBBLE

IS MME STEFA FRENCH?

NO, WHY?

SHE SOMETIMES TALKS WITH OTHER TEACHERS IN FRENCH

OH!

SO THAT WE DON'T UNDERSTAND

DO YOU WANT TO KNOW WHAT SHE SAID?

NOD # NOD

SHE SAID THAT ISMAEL MAY DROWN IN ALL THAT KINDNESS

Whisper Whisper Whisper Whisper

Hi Hi Hi Hi Hi Hi Hi

CHILDREN!

CHATTER CHATTER CHATTER CHATTER

IT'S TIME TO CATCH UP WITH

OUR HOUSE NEWSPAPER, "THE LITTLE REVIEW"

chapter
XI

SO, WHAT DO WE DO?

C'MON KAJTEK, TELL US!

UHHH

UM... SO, FIRST, I GUESS YOU HAVE TO THINK OF SOMETHING REALLY HARD...

AND THEN

SAY SOME- THING

OR...

I DON'T KNOW...

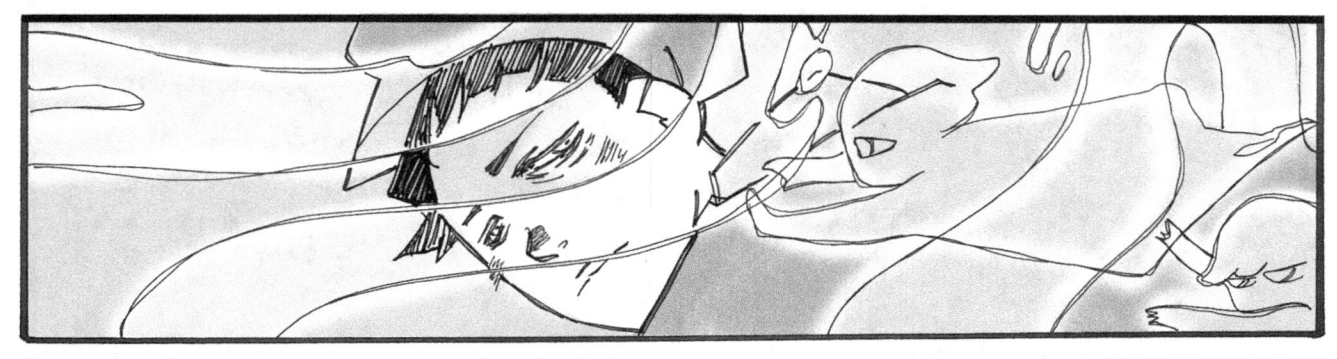

SILENCE!

WHEN I WAS LYING ON THE FLOOR, I SAW HOW YOU BOTH

USED MAGIC TO BRING ME BACK

REALLY?!

BUT I STILL THINK YOU BEHAVED LIKE DOLTS

AND I HAD TO SUFFER FOR IT

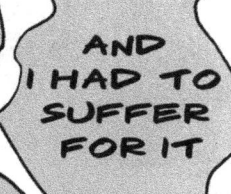

WE CAN DO MAGIC!

...

chapter XII

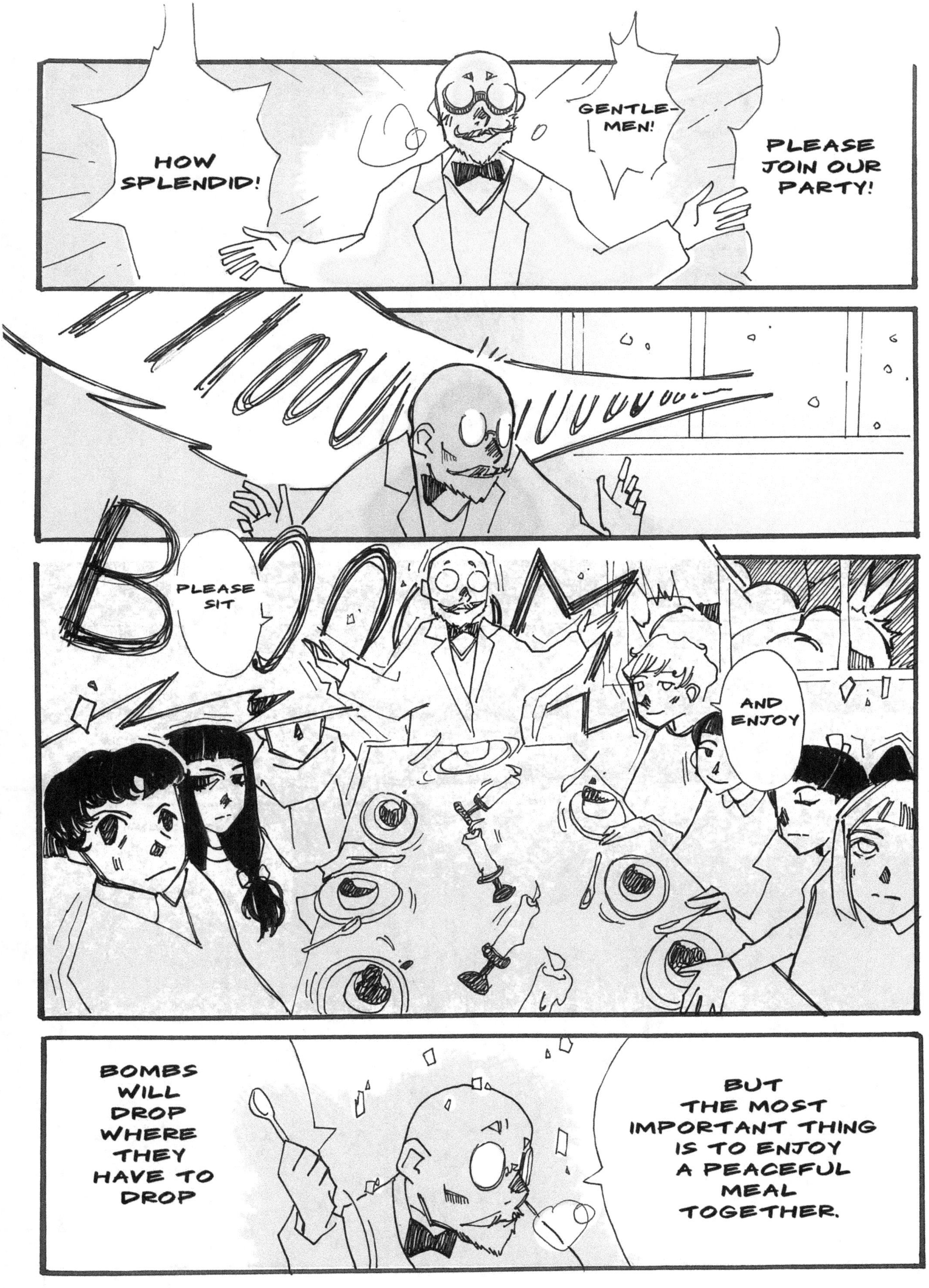

chapter XIII

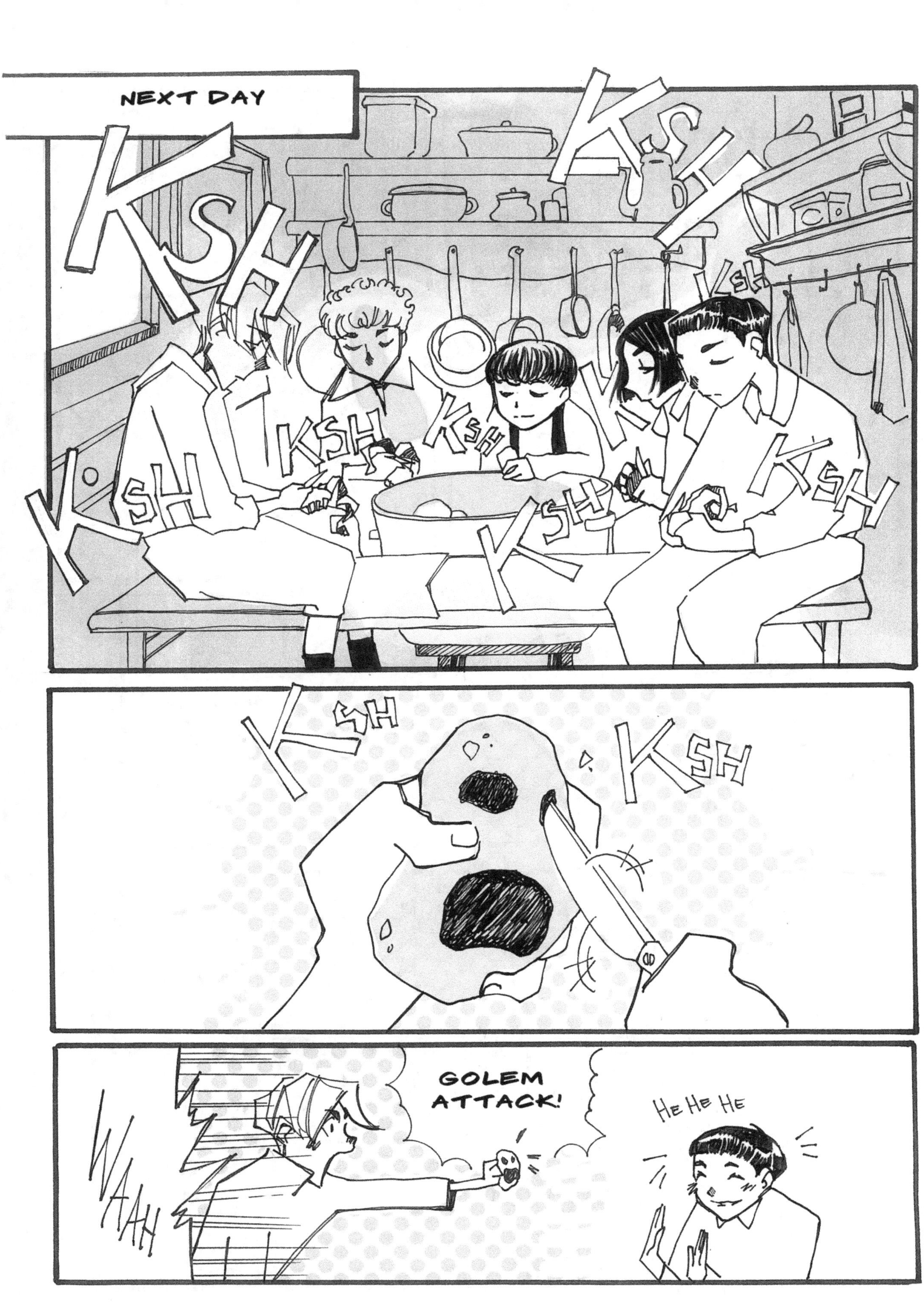

NEXT DAY

GOLEM ATTACK!

HE HE HE

chapter XIV

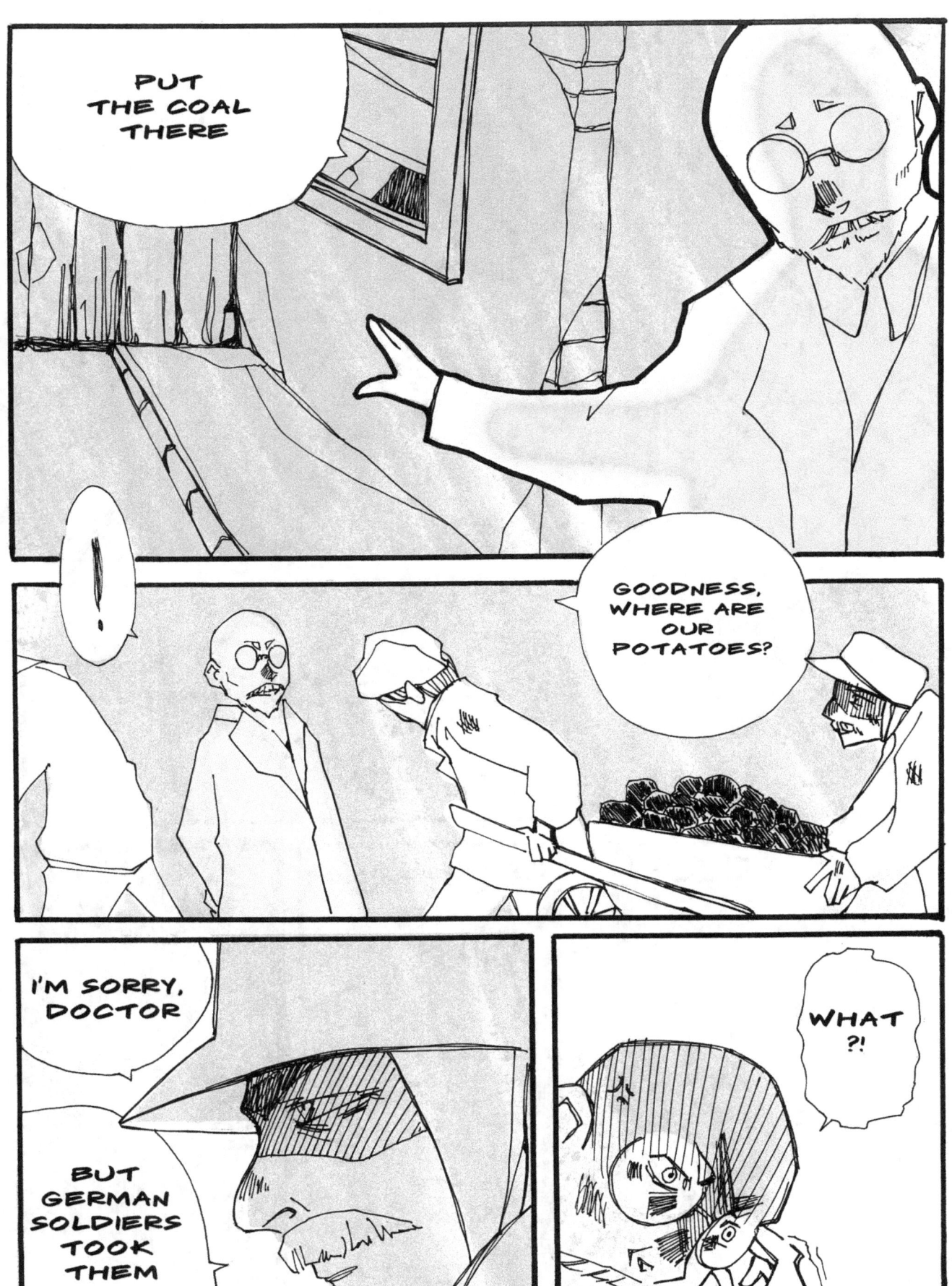

chapter
XV

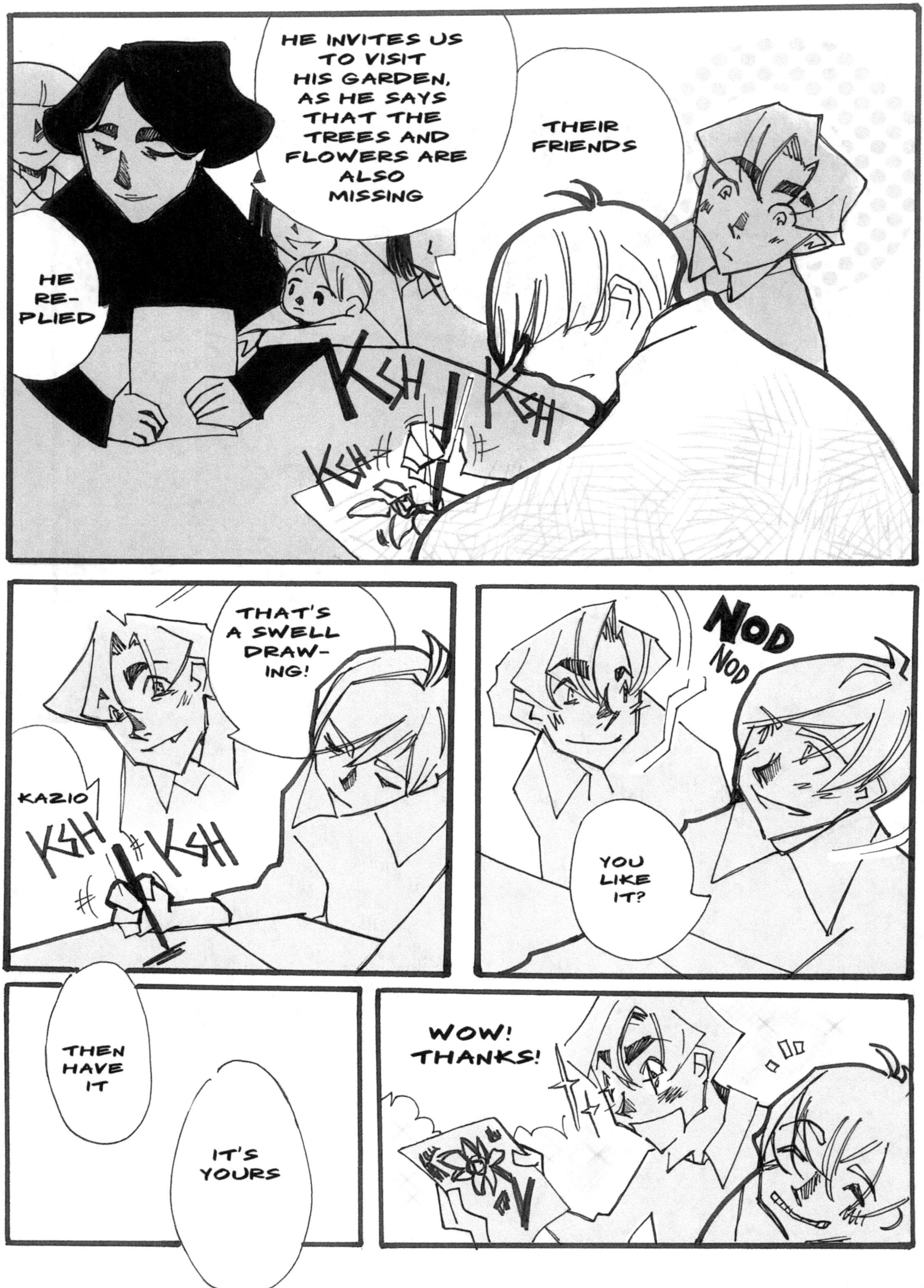

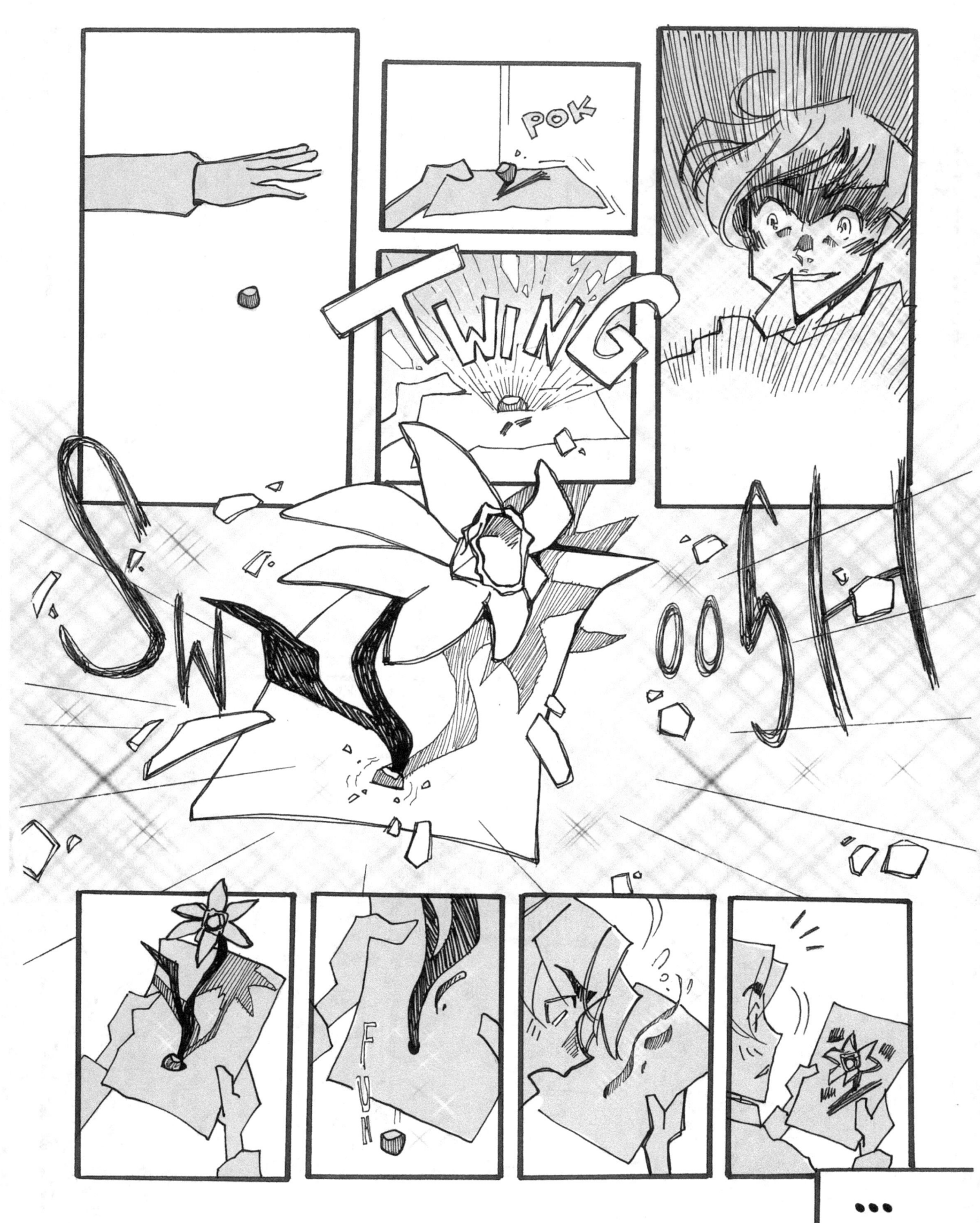

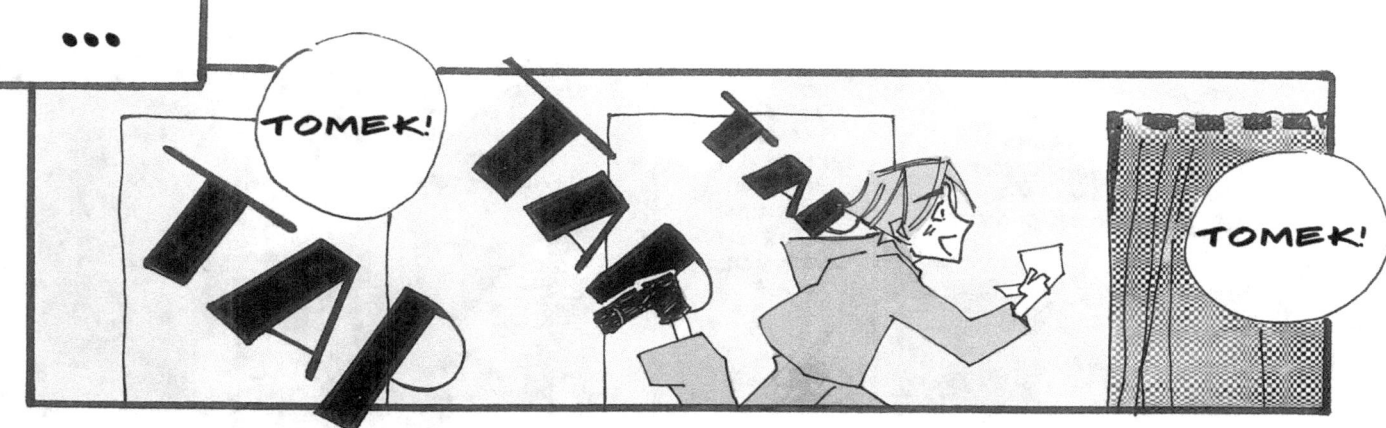

WE'RE TESTING OUR NEW MOVIE THEATRE AND WATCHING SLIDES FROM SUMMER HOLIDAYS

THESE ARE PHOTOS FROM SUMMER CAMP IN "RÓŻYCZ-KA"

THE OWNER OF THE BUILDING CALLED IT AFTER HIS LATE DAUGHTER

AND THEN DONATED IT TO THE ORPHAN-AGE

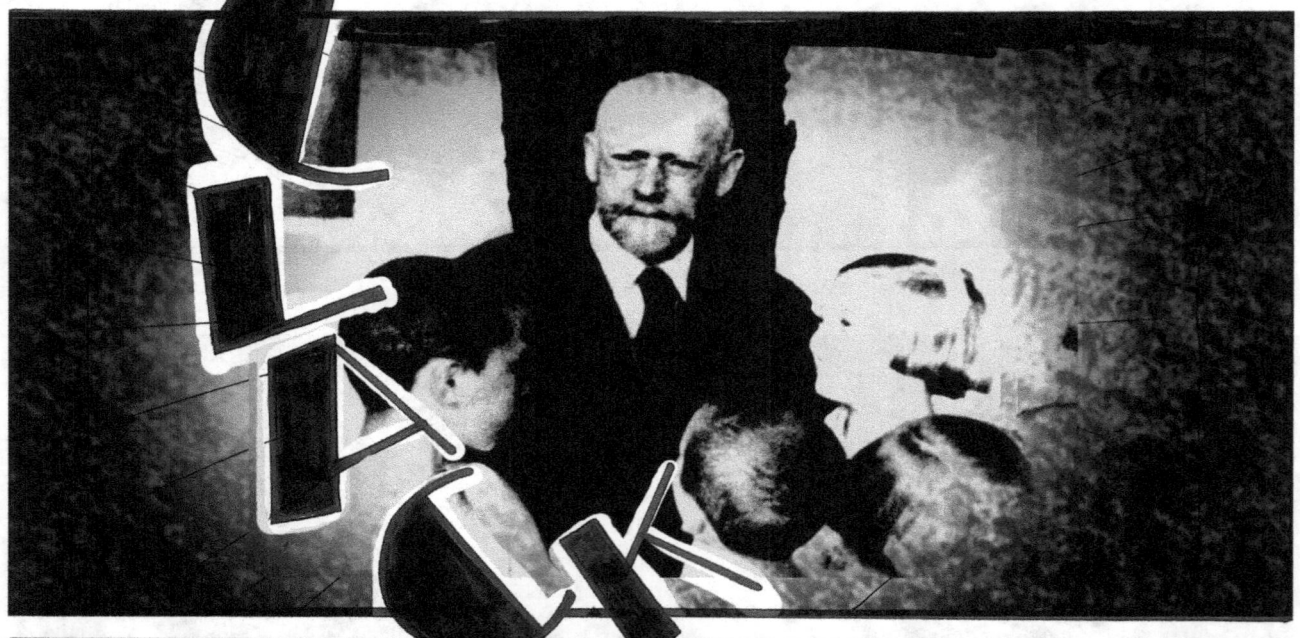

...

...

chapter XVI

A MONTH LATER
SHUF
SHUF
UGH, I HAVE A HOR-RIBLE FEVER
AND MY HEAD HURTS SO MUCH
I THINK I'M GONNA BE SICK
I CAN'T SLEEP WELL
AND I CAN'T SLEEP AT ALL
I DON'T HAVE ANY ENERGY
AND I CAN'T FOCUS ON ANYTHING!

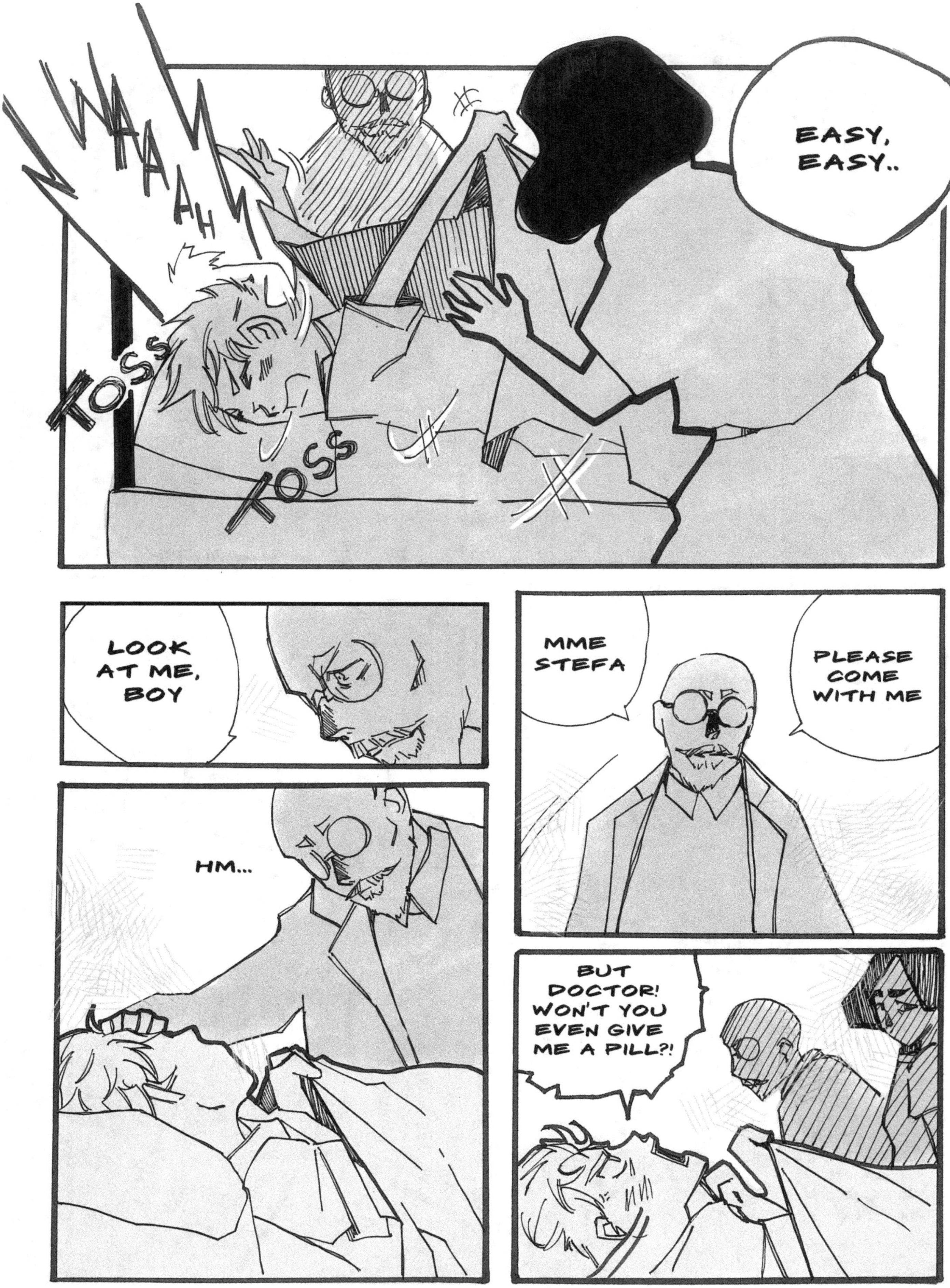

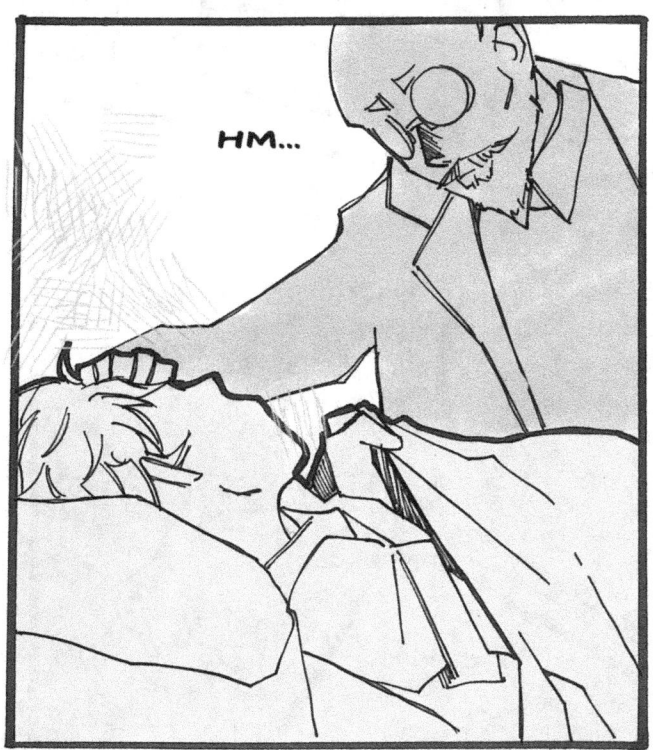

THAT'S ENOUGH!!!

IS THIS A CHILDREN'S HOUSE

OR A HOSPICE?!

YOU HAVE SUCH COMFORTABLE LIVES IN HERE AND ALL YOU DO IS COMPETE ABOUT YOUR AILMENTS!

YOU DON'T CARE ABOUT ANYTHING BUT YOUR OWN HEALTH!

IF YOU SAW THESE CHILDREN ON THE STREETS...

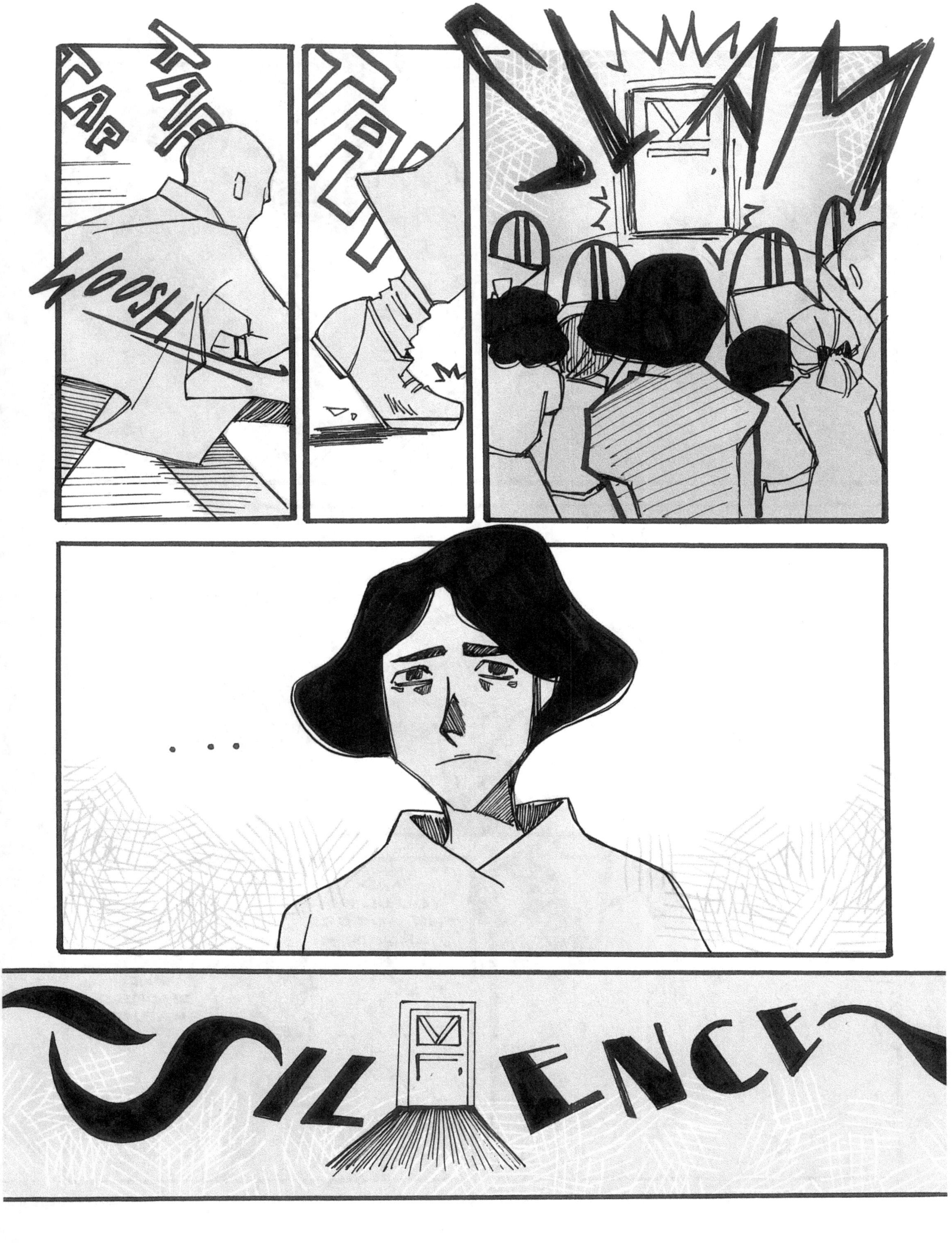

chapter XVII

LET THE PLAY BEGIN

THE MAD KING'S
HENCHMEN KIDNAP
A PRINCESS

AND THE GOOD KING IS
SO BROKEN HEARTED
THAT HE DECIDES TO
ABANDON HIS KINGDOM

The Head of the Warsaw Ghetto Jewish
Council commits suicide after the
commencement of mass extermination
of Jews.

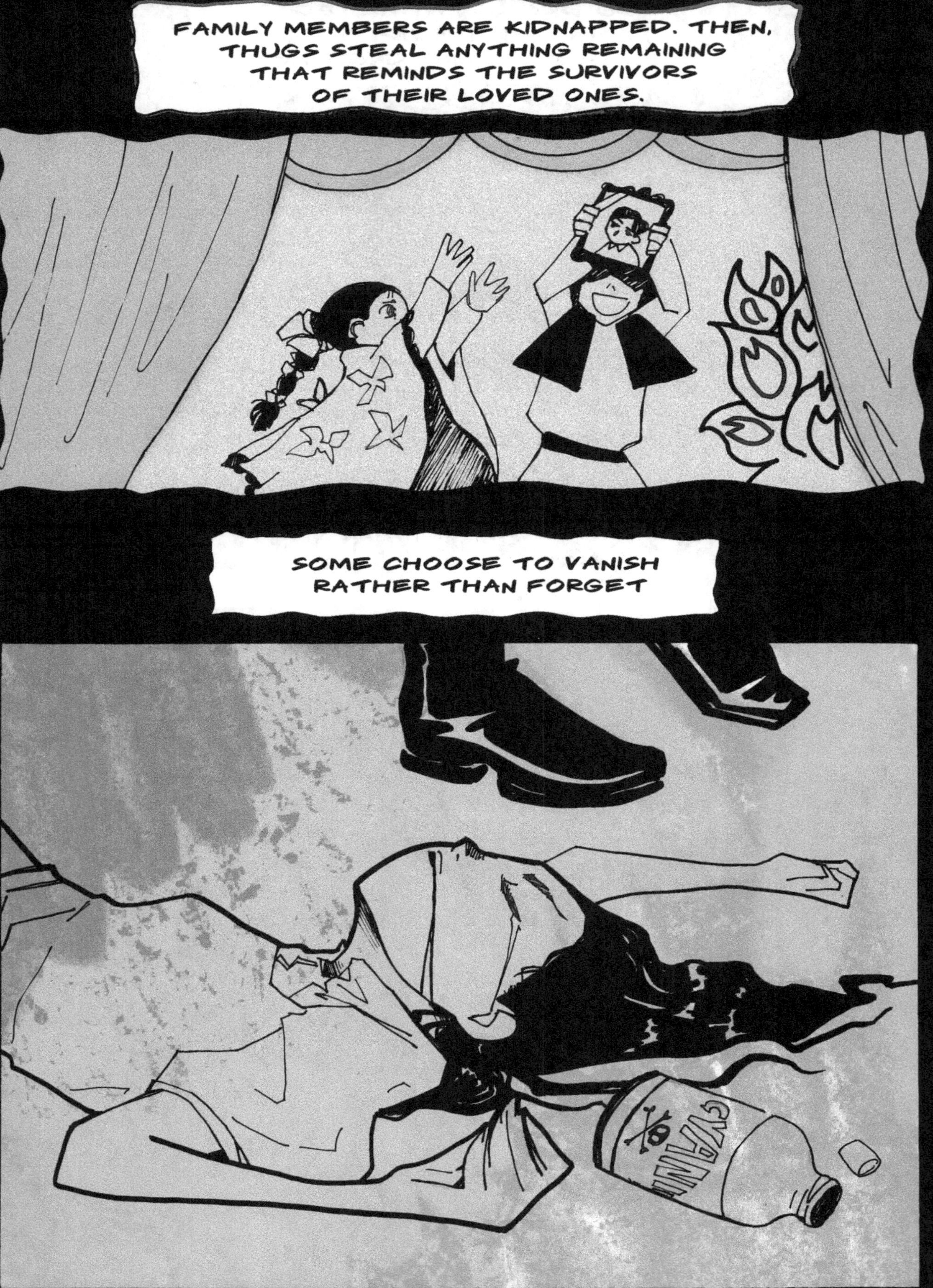

FAMILY MEMBERS ARE KIDNAPPED. THEN, THUGS STEAL ANYTHING REMAINING THAT REMINDS THE SURVIVORS OF THEIR LOVED ONES.

SOME CHOOSE TO VANISH RATHER THAN FORGET

A PLAGUE DECIMATES THE KINGDOM'S CHILDREN. BUT THEN, WITH THE HELP OF A TOOTH FAIRY, THE PRINCE BUILDS A CASTLE WHERE ALL THE CHILDREN CAN TAKE REFUGE

FINALLY, THE PRINCE FINDS THE PRINCESS.
HE SAVES HER BY SACRIFICING HIS LIFE,
SO HE MUST REMAIN IN THE UNDERWORLD.
BUT THEN: HE FINDS A PORTAL! AND
IT LEADS HIM FROM THE UNDERWORLD
TO A WORLD WHERE THERE'S NO PLACE
FOR MAD KINGS.

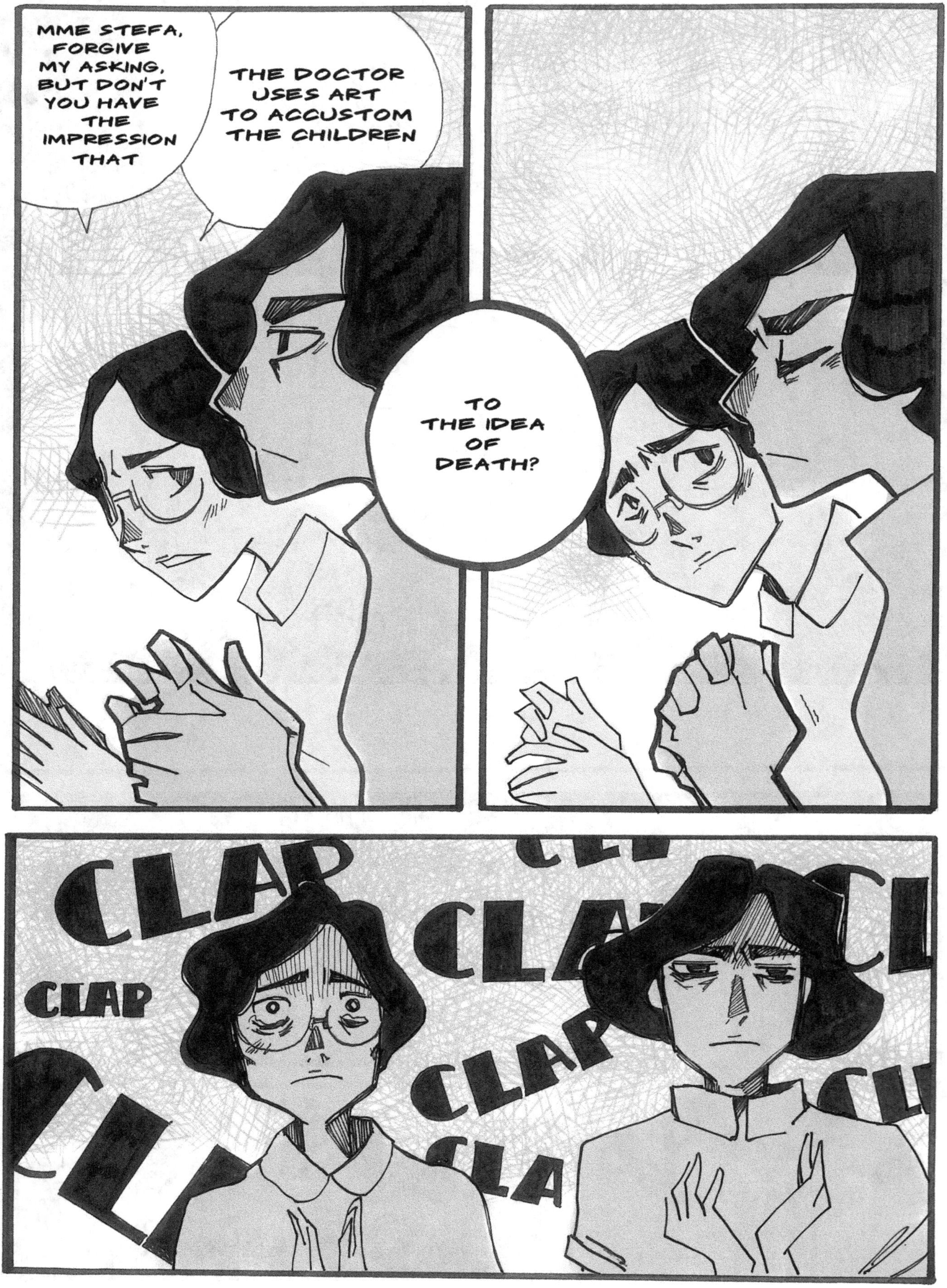

chapter XVIII

*EXTERMINATION CAMP NEAR THE VILLAGE OF TREBLINKA, 50 MILES FROM WARSAW

* CULTURAL ASSIMILATION AND SOCIAL INTEGRATION OF JEWS IN THE LOCAL CULTURE

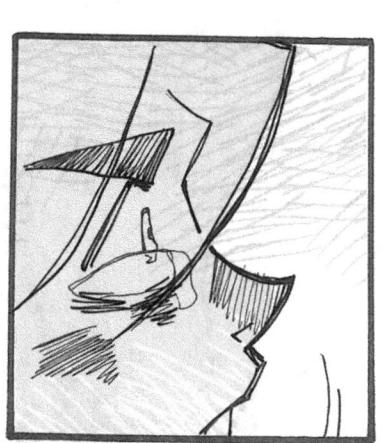

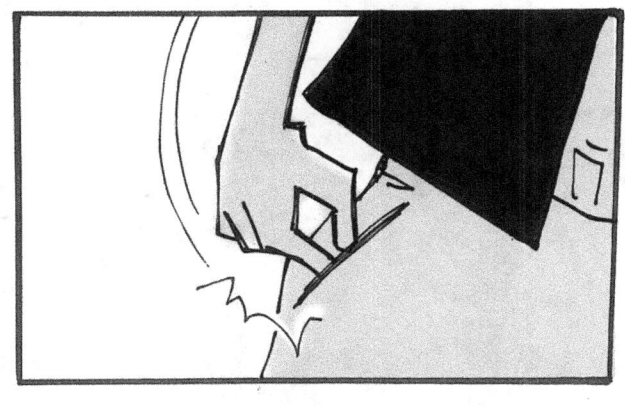

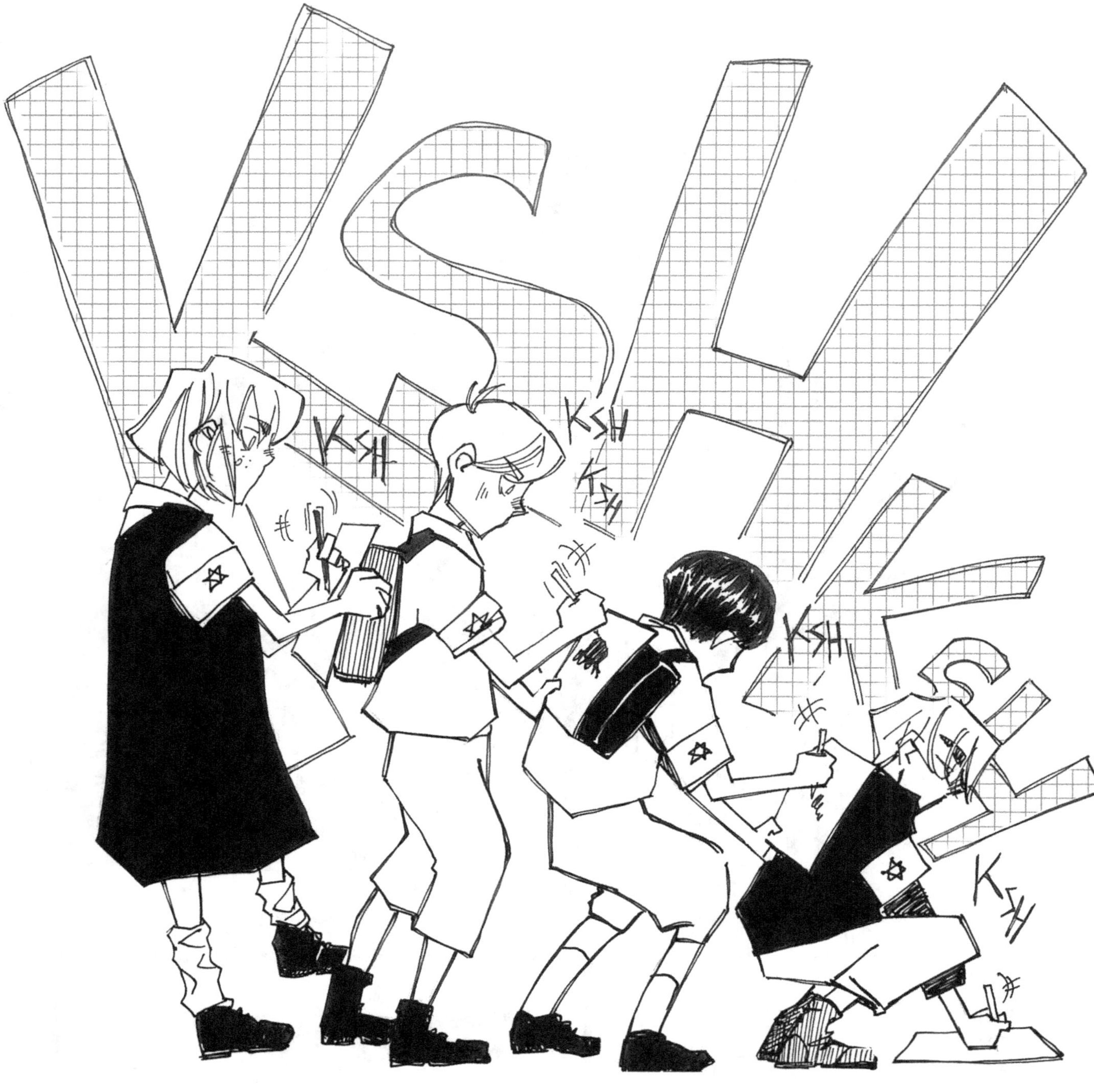

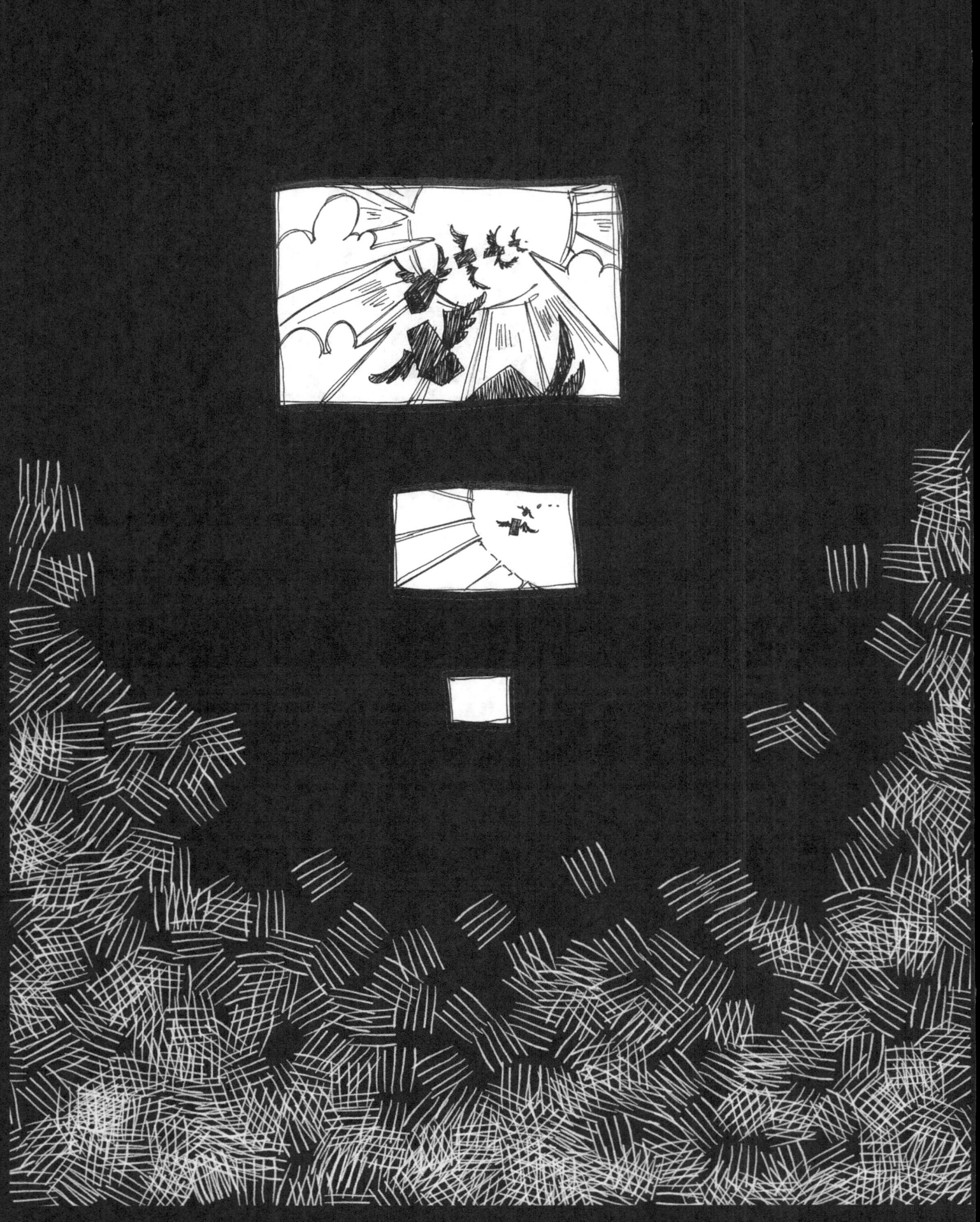

ONE GIRL SAID THAT, WHEN SHE WAS VISITING HER GRANDPA

IN HIS HOUSE IN A VILLAGE

SHE SAW A BOY BEING CARRIED INTO THE RAISING SUN

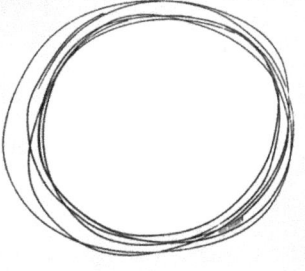

ON THE SHOULDERS OF A TREMENDOUS GIANT

THE END